"He said you needed watching and he shouldn't have let you come."

Kit looked down. "Charles will stoop to any level to achieve want he wants."

"What does he want?" Ross prodded her.

"He wants Andy to be the son he lost!"

"There's more to it than that for him to phone the ranch asking for one of us in charge."

A tortured moan escaped her. "No—I mean there is a reason, but it's not what you think."

"Then explain it to me."

"I—I don't know where to start," she stammered. "It's complicated."

"Nightmares usually are. I've got all night and you're my responsibility while you're here."

"I don't want you mixed up in this."

His temper flared. "I already am. Does he have a case against you for being an unfit mother?"

He heard her sharp intake of breath. "In his mind he does," she said.

Ross felt as if he'd been kicked in the gut.

Dear Reader,

The heroine in my story *Her Wyoming Hero* finds herself in a situation where she's being controlled and manipulated and can no longer tolerate it. To change her life, and the life of her son, she will have to summon all her inner strength and courage to do what she needs to do.

Kit began her marriage naive and starry-eyed, but that state of bliss soon passed, and her struggle began. At the end of this struggle she emerges a strong, capable woman ready to stand on her own two feet. But when she meets Ross Livingston, she's faced with a new, unexpected challenge and doesn't want history to repeat itself. I hope you'll find this story compelling and cheer Kit to the end. She deserves a happy ending, but how will she get there? That's for you to discover.

Enjoy!

Rebecca Winters

HER
WYOMING
HERO

—

REBECCA WINTERS

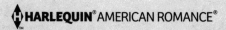

Recycling programs
for this product may
not exist in your area.

ISBN-13: 978-0-373-75475-5

HER WYOMING HERO

Copyright © 2013 by Rebecca Winters

Printed in U.S.A.

ABOUT THE AUTHOR

Rebecca Winters, whose family of four children has now swelled to include five beautiful grandchildren, lives in Salt Lake City, Utah, in the land of the Rocky Mountains. With canyons and high alpine meadows full of wildflowers nearby, she never runs out of places to explore. These spaces, plus her favorite vacation spots in Europe, often end up as backgrounds for her romance novels. Writing is her passion, along with her family and church. Rebecca loves to hear from readers. If you wish to email her, please visit her website, www.cleanromances.com.

Books by Rebecca Winters

HARLEQUIN AMERICAN ROMANCE

*Undercover Heroes
**Daddy Dude Ranch

To all strong women everywhere with the courage of their convictions to make a difference in their lives despite the odds.

Chapter One

July 10
Bar Harbor, Maine

Kit read the letter postmarked from Wyoming one more time, positive it had been sent to her by mistake. The honor to her deceased marine husband thrilled her, but didn't make sense.

Dear Mrs. Wentworth,
My name is Carson Lundgren. You don't know me from Adam. I served as a marine in Afghanistan before I got out of the service.

When we returned to the U.S., I, along with Buck Summerhays and Ross Livingston, fellow retired marines, went into business at the Teton Valley Dude Ranch. Our idea was to offer what we could to the families of the fallen soldiers from our various units.

Your courageous husband, Winston Pettigrew Wentworth, served our country with honor and distinction. Now we'd like to honor him by offering you and your son Andrew an expense free, one week vacation at the dude ranch anytime in

August. We'll pay for your airfare and any other travel expenses.

You're welcome to contact your husband's division commander, Colonel Hodges, at the phone number below. His office helped us obtain your address. If you're interested and have questions, please call our office. We've also listed our web address, where you'll find a brochure with more details about the ranch. We'll also be happy to email you any additional information.

Please know how anxious we are to give something back to you after his great sacrifice.

With warmest regards,

Carson Lundgren.

His words touched Kit beyond measure, but she was the daughter-in-law of Charles Wentworth, an East Coast billionaire. Such an honor should go to a grief-stricken family whose loss of the husband and father from the home would have affected them financially.

Without hesitation she reached for the phone. In a few minutes she was able to speak to Colonel Hodges. When he came on the line she explained the reason for her call.

"I think this invitation is the most wonderful thing that has happened to me and Andy since the funeral. But I fear it was sent by mistake. There are so many soldiers who've died in this ghastly war. They've left families who are now struggling to make a decent living without them. I'm not in that category and wouldn't dream of accepting this generous offer."

"Mrs. Wentworth, I don't think you understand.

These retired marines out in Wyoming know who you are. I've talked with them at length. They admired your husband for serving when he could have stayed home and enjoyed all the privileges of his life, but this invitation is about something much more important. A rich man can suffer as much as a poor one, don't you agree?"

"Well, yes. Of course, but—"

"They want you and your son to know that your husband's heroism hasn't gone unnoticed. Perhaps you don't realize that these men are trying to deal with their own grief and the many losses they've seen.

"This isn't about money. It's about helping you find a way out of your grief any way they can. During your week there, they would like to get to know your son and talk to him about his father's great sacrifice. The truth is, they need healing, too. Does that help you to understand and accept their invitation?"

Kit was so humbled by his comments, she could hardly speak. "Yes," she whispered. "You've given me a new perspective about a lot of things. I appreciate your kindness more than you know. Thank you, Colonel."

After hanging up, she stared into space while she digested the full impact of Winn's commander's words. He could have no idea what this meant to her. For once she and Andy were being offered something that hadn't been prescribed and paid for by her father-in-law.

Little did the colonel know she and Andy had both been grieving in silence for years—long before Winn's death. Now the loss of his father had caused a change in her withdrawn and morose son. Lately he'd been acting out in negative ways, and Kit was so heartsick for him she didn't know where to turn.

This letter was one he needed to see. It would make him proud of his father, and a trip to a ranch out west would be something neither of them had ever experienced before. The idea of getting away from her grieving in-laws for a whole week where she could be fully in charge of her son filled her with guilty excitement.

While Andy was still at his piano lesson, she hurried through the house to her father-in-law's den. It was almost time for dinner. She needed to talk to him before she mentioned anything to Andy.

She found him at his desk, where he was studying some papers. "Charles?" Since the day Winn had brought her to the Wentworth mansion after their wedding ten years ago, her father-in-law had told her to call him that. "Can I talk to you for a minute?"

He lifted his graying head. "If this is about that notion of yours to move out on your own, we've had this conversation too many times before. It's out of the question."

Winn had wanted to live with his parents following their marriage, and he had dismissed Kit's questions about living away from the mansion. Now that her husband was gone, she intended to get a job and a place of her own for her and Andy. But she had to figure out all the details first before she told her son what they were going to do. Once she'd discussed it with Andy, then she'd find the right moment to tell her in-laws.

"No, I'm here about this letter I received." She placed it on the desk in front of him.

He put on his glasses. After reading it, he cleared his throat. Mr. Lundgren's words had gotten to her father-in-law, too. "I'm pleased they would like to honor Winston this way, but you can't think of accepting. This offer is for widows who have no money."

She told him about her conversation with Colonel Hodges. "He helped me understand that going to the ranch is for those retired marines, too, so I'd like to accept. I'll let Mr. Lundgren know we'll be coming for the last week of August."

"You can't go then. We have other plans."

Her cheeks grew warm battling him for every inch of ground. "But I'm in charge of the Cosgriff Memorial Library benefit. There's so much to do throughout the beginning of August, I won't be able to get away until it's over. When Andy realizes these men want to do something wonderful for him—because of his father's heroism—I'm hoping it will help him to feel a little happier before he starts school. Please. You and Florence take the rest of the family on that cruise of the fjords without us and enjoy yourselves."

"What do you mean, without us?" Florence spoke behind her.

Kit turned around to face her always stylish mother-in-law. "Andy and I are going to take a trip to Wyoming the last week of August. We're to be the special guests of some retired marines who want to honor Winn by inviting us to their dude ranch. It's all there in the letter." Her eyes darted to the desk.

"Have you forgotten we've had this trip planned for months?"

"No." *What to do...* "I could call Mr. Lundgren right now and find out if it will be all right if we come the first week of September. We could leave on a Friday

and come back the next Saturday. Now if you'll excuse
me, I'll go get Andy ready for dinner."

August 31
Teton Valley Dude Ranch

"You've got a faraway look in your eye, Ross." A cough
had preceded the statement. "Is it possible there's a
woman on your mind?"

On this beautiful Saturday morning, Ross Livingston
and his partner Carson Lundgren had been inspecting
the border of Carson's Teton Valley Dude Ranch, located fifteen minutes from Jackson, Wyoming. They
could exercise the horses and talk business at the same
time.

Buck Summerhayes, the other retired marine making
up their triumvirate, had just married a woman who had
come to the ranch in July as their invited guest. At the
moment he was understandably detained, so he couldn't
attend this meeting. Carson had married in June, leaving Ross the lone bachelor.

"I'm thinking a lot of things, but not about a woman."
They'd ridden to the eastern section of the property
away from the forest that provided spectacular blocks
of color. It was the last day of August. Another week of
temperatures in the lower seventies, and then it would
be fall. Carson had told his friend from a more southern
clime that the cold came a little earlier here, so enjoy
the warm weather while they could.

Ross's dark brown eyes followed the flat, treeless
sweep of sage with no sign of civilization in sight.

He loved every square inch of this fabulous property watched over by the magnificent Grand Teton.

"If you're having reservations about our recent decision to keep the dude ranch running year round, I'm open to anything you have to say. This place hasn't operated in the black for years. It's nothing new."

That's what worried Ross. Though their regular dude ranch business was growing, he wanted Carson to be able to get out from under the constant worry of making ends meet, a problem Ross had never been forced to deal with.

"No reservations. Like you, I'm anxious to keep this going for a year to see how we do in our venture."

Turning the working ranch into a dude ranch had been Carson's idea when the three of them had been hospitalized together at Walter Reed in January. He'd inherited it from his deceased grandfather and wanted to make it into a profitable business.

The guys had gotten together and pooled their resources. Once they'd been discharged from the hospital, they'd started making their dream a reality. Besides building new cabins and making renovations to the ranch house and other structures, they'd created a website and done enough advertising to attract people from all over the country who wanted to experience life on a ranch. It had been a major endeavor that had included the hiring of staff.

Throughout all that process they'd also discussed how to manage their guilt for surviving the war and had come up with the idea to give a week's free vacation once a month to a son or a daughter of a fallen soldier. To be a substitute daddy for a week to the fatherless children had been a part of their goal, but there was much more to it.

The guys hoped that in helping the mothers and children explore the outdoors on horseback and take in the wonders of the rugged natural world, they'd let go of some of their grief and learn that there was joy in being alive despite their loss. The children needed to know their fathers were good men who'd made an invaluable contribution to their country and would always be remembered. Hopefully the activities the ranch provided would help restore their confidence.

So far the "daddy dude ranch" experiment, as they called it, had produced wonders far beyond anyone's expectations. Not only had the two women and children who'd come this summer found new joy here, his partners had lost their hearts to them and there'd been two marriages.

Ross found it uncanny what had happened, marveling over the happy coincidences. Now there was one more military widow with her son due to arrive this evening—Kathryn and Andrew Wentworth. Their husband and father happened to have been the son of Charles Cavanaugh Wentworth from Maine, an established and wealthy East Coast family.

According to Colonel Hodges, Mrs. Wentworth had been hesitant to accept the guys' invitation, feeling it should go to a family in financial need. That piece of information did her credit, but her husband's exceptional valor had decided them on giving him and his family the special recognition he deserved.

Ross had still to decide what it was going to be like taking care of two people who'd been given every luxury life had to offer. Having been born a Livingston of the billionaire oil barons of Texas, he knew firsthand the kind of society she and her son had come from. He would reserve judgment, however, until after he'd spent some time with them.

As for now, he was excited about an idea he wanted to explore with Carson. It had been percolating in his mind for a long time, but he hadn't wanted to bring it up until he could see how well their dude ranch business had been doing.

"So, what gives?" Carson prodded him.

Ross would have answered, but like Carson and Buck, he had a cough they'd picked up in Afghanistan that had ended their military careers. This morning there was a hint of smoke in the air from a forest fire in nearby Yellowstone. It had aggravated their coughs. He pulled out his inhaler prescribed by the doctor. Pretty soon he got some relief, but the medicine had a tendency to make him sleepy, something he had to fight while they were out on the range.

When he finally caught his breath, Ross began. "Correct me if I'm wrong, but didn't you once tell me your great great grandfather obtained the mineral rights to this place before the government could get their hands on them?"

Carson eyed him with curiosity. "I did."

"I've been giving it a lot of thought since Sublette and Fremont Counties bordering you have been seeing a boom in natural gas."

"That's right. You graduated in petroleum engineering. You think there's gas under my land?" he asked before letting go with a cough.

"With more and more energy companies springing up around Lander and Thermopolis, I think there's a pretty good possibility you're living on top of a big pocket of it here in Teton County. Wyoming has the second largest proven natural gas reserve in the U.S. behind Texas."

I ought to know, he thought with a grimace. His last name was synonymous with oil in the Lone Star State, where he'd been raised.

"The money you'd derive from a producing well could keep the ranch solvent for years to come. It's just a thought." One Ross would like to see happen for his friend.

"A few years ago my grandfather told me he'd been approached by a gas company, but he wouldn't hear of doing anything about it."

"I can understand that. Wyoming is a pristine environment that has been underexplored and underexploited. I'm sure he wanted to keep it that way."

"He feared the onslaught of progress."

"You can't blame him. But the ever-increasing demand for gas in the U.S. has led to a quadrupling of the price, causing companies in Russia and Venezuela, both big natural gas suppliers, to have shut off access to foreign companies. The same in the Gulf of Mexico where easy-to-drill reserves have been depleted. Progress has made its way to your door."

Carson pushed his cowboy hat back on his head. "You're talking about drilling for it right here?"

"This is the flattest uninhabited section of your land away from people and animals. Bringing in a road over this section would cause the least amount of disturbance to the environment and would be virtually invisible. Naturally I can't give you proof there's gas here without doing some preliminary drilling."

His friend was quiet for a minute. "Wouldn't that cost a ton of money I don't have?"

Ross nodded. "But I have some savings I can draw from. It would be my way of investing in your ranch to give you something back after what you've done for me. Then I'd feel a real part of it."

"You already are," Carson answered solemnly.

"I'd like to do more for you."

After a pause Carson asked, "What all would be involved?"

Ross was pleased his friend was at least listening to his proposal. "Wyoming's gas is unconventional. It doesn't sit in easy pools above oil, but thousands of feet beneath the earth in pockets of sandstone and coal formations. If the gas is there, the steel pipe will have to drive 11,000 feet into the ground to capture it.

"One good thing. Nowadays gas companies can put the derricks down on mats instead of the ground in order to preserve the top soil and roots. But there's no way around the fact that there are still a lot of negatives, and always will be."

"You've got me thinking," Carson said as Ross's phone rang, interrupting their conversation.

When he saw it was the ranch calling, he clicked on. "Hey, Willy. What's up?" The part-time mechanic helped run the front desk.

"There's been another change in the Wentworths' itinerary you need to know about."

He coughed. "What's that?" Earlier in the week their

latest invited guest had already indicated she wouldn't be able to make it on Friday and would come Saturday instead.

"The fax says she and her son will be flying into Jackson Hole at three p.m."

He frowned while Carson looked on. "I wonder why they aren't coming in on the flight we arranged." They weren't supposed to be due in until six-thirty this evening.

"I don't know. Since you're out touring the ranch, do you want me to go for them?"

Ross checked his watch. There was time to get back and shower if he and Carson left now. "No." This was his responsibility. "I'll do it. Thanks for the heads-up, Willy." He clicked off.

"What's going on?"

"Mrs. Wentworth will be here at three instead of six-thirty. I need to get going."

"I'll ride with you. I promised to spend part of the day showing Johnny how to ride bareback."

"That boy gets better every day."

"He's a natural."

"Just like his new dad." Ross smiled at his friend. "Carson? Give what we talked about some thought and let me know later."

"Why don't you get a few bids together and we'll go from there."

"I'm going to get on it pronto."

They took off at a gallop. Carson hadn't said no. Drilling a hole from start to finish would take a month. It would be better to do it before winter set in. Ross would arrange to meet an oil engineer out here on Monday. Then he could present it to Carson with more information to back up his idea.

But right now he had other things on his mind. For the next week he would have his hands full entertaining a nine-year-old boy who'd lost his father and was grieving.

Ross hoped he was as sweet as Johnny Lundgren, Carson's newly adopted seven-year-old son. The boy had charmed everyone on the ranch with his curiosity and good nature, and had walked right into his friend's heart. For that matter so had Buck's new stepdaughter, Jenny. Ross was crazy about both the kids.

Once they'd returned their horses to the barn, Carson took off for his new house, the one Buck had built for him, Tracy and Johnny on the property near the Snake River. Buck came from a family who owned a construction business. As for Ross, he drove the Jeep back to the main ranch house to get cleaned up.

Since Buck had moved downstairs with his wife, Alex, and her granddaughter, Jenny, Ross had the whole top floor of the place to himself. For the first time since his return from Afghanistan last January, he was aware of his "aloneness" and didn't like it.

With his mood becoming decidedly morose on that score, Ross was lucky he had guests to pick up.

Carson's earlier question about a possible woman on Ross's mind had hit a nerve. *One day, I'll have a family of my own.*

THE JET FROM Denver taxied to a stop at the Jackson airport. Kit's heart hammered in her ears. She undid the seat belt and got to her feet, glancing at her desperately unhappy son who was still sleepy from the medicine she'd given him for air sickness.

This was it. The day she'd been praying for had come.

Freedom.

Joy of joys, she and Andy were the *only* ones in the Wentworth family invited to stay on the Wyoming ranch. They would have a whole week to themselves to get closer and make plans for the future. When they left, they would be going to a new place to live. She had it all arranged. If her in-laws wanted to remain in her life and Andy's, they would have to deal with her move and accept it.

The letter inviting them here had served as a stepping-stone to their new life. When these retired marines had shown such kindness and generosity, she'd been moved to tears, not only for Andy's sake, but her own. Not that her son hadn't had a different attitude than hers when she'd first told him.

"I'm *not* going." He'd sounded so much like his obstinate deceased father, with that same mulish tone of voice that often crept in these days. "I don't want to go anywhere."

"Honey, this is a great honor for all of us. Think of it—these military men are trying to show you how much they care what your dad did to save lives."

"I don't want to go." He'd kicked the end of his bed in anger.

"Andy—I never want to see you do that again!"

"But a dude ranch sounds stupid!" He'd turned away from her.

To her horror, he was becoming more and more unmanageable lately. He hadn't seemed to enjoy the cruise vacation at all. His grandparents were so cold and controlling. Winn's death only served to have brought a permanent winter into their lives. Though she'd been out of love with her husband for years, she ached for Andy and what he was going through, after losing his father.

"How could a vacation like this be stupid?"

"They're a bunch of lame marines. I *hate* them!"

Kit thought she understood. To Andy, a letter from the marines represented death and was a terrible reminder of the many months over the years his father had been away on deployment.

This trip would be the first time in years the two of them were completely on their own without the family there to run Andy's life. Though he'd finally stopped fighting her over the decision to bring him to Wyoming, she saw the deep misery in his eyes. Unfortunately, her darling son had no idea how much more misery was in store for him if they didn't make the break from his grandparents, who were swallowing them alive.

Winn and his parents had decided years ago that when Andy turned nine, he would be sent to a special elite boarding school located an hour away from Bar Harbor where discipline was strictly enforced. He'd be granted a weekend pass twice a month if he kept up his grades. He was due to start school there in mid-September.

Winn had been sent to the same school at his age and expected that for Andy. It was tradition among the Wentworths, one of the founding families of Maine.

Her husband had paid the $50,000 deposit years earlier to reserve his place.

It didn't matter that he was no longer alive. Andy's grandfather would carry out his son's wishes and ignore hers. But Andy was *her* son and her *raison d'être*. When Kit had objected because she wanted Andy at home with her, he'd stated the matter was closed.

Since his death the tension at the Wentworth mansion had grown much worse. The out-of-the-blue letter from the ranch was a miracle, and had helped give her the jump start she needed to make some serious decisions. She knew that for her to move out and get a life of her own would be a huge change for both of them—not to mention traumatic for her in-laws.

That's why she needed this week in Wyoming first to prepare Andy. It would mean treading carefully to broach this plan with her son. If his anger grew any worse, he could possibly require professional help. What if in time Andy turned into his grandfather, outgrowing the sweetness of his nature he'd been born with?

"Honey?" she said quietly. "We've arrived."

His eyes blinked open. They were a lighter gray than Winn's. His cheek had a line indented into it from lying against the seat. When he slept he became her dear son again, instead of the impossible nine-year-old child she no longer knew.

"Do you need to go to the bathroom before we leave the plane?"

"No." His rude answer resonated in the jet's interior. He unfastened his seat belt and got up with a scowl on his face. "I told you I don't want to be here."

She was sick for him, knowing he was a volcano

ready to explode from all of the pain and emotion he held inside. Kit had lost her influence over him years ago, but she was his mother and he needed her. Even if he wasn't aware of it.

Because the family had her trapped in an emotional vise of guilt, she'd been ineffectual in dealing with him. Now, that was going to change—she couldn't live under the same roof with her in-laws any longer. She had to leave, and when she did there'd be no going back.

With his shoulders slumped, Andy started down the aisle behind the other passengers without saying anything else. She grabbed her handbag and followed him to the exit. When they reached the inside of the terminal, Kit saw a cowboy in well-worn boots striding toward them with unconscious male authority. A brown Western shirt and jeans covered his tall, fit physique.

The striking male looked to be in his early thirties. He tipped back his sand-colored cowboy hat, revealing a widow's peak of raven-black hair. There were no rings on his fingers. "Mrs. Wentworth?"

As she moved closer his dark brown eyes sized her up. They were neither admiring or leering, one of the two looks she was used to receiving from men. For the first time since she could remember, she saw a guarded look coming from the stranger's eyes and wondered why.

"Are you Mr. Lundgren?"

"No. I'm Ross Livingston, his business partner." He possessed a deep voice, but his civil response didn't have the Western twang she'd expected.

"I remember your name from the letter. It's a great pleasure to meet you. This is my son, Andy. I'm sorry if you had trouble meeting this earlier plane. We've been in Norway and caught a flight out of New York to Denver that put us in here ahead of schedule."

"No problem at all. We're glad you arrived safely."

Still feeling unsettled by the way he'd been looking at her, she said, "We're very honored you would choose our family when there are so many others affected by the war. Andy's father would be incredibly proud."

"After your husband's sacrifice, we consider it our pleasure." He stepped forward to shake their hands but focused his attention on Andy. "Welcome to the Teton Valley Dude Ranch, son." After a cough he asked, "Have you ever been to Wyoming?"

"No." The peeved sound that came out of Andy was totally mortifying to her.

Kit glanced at their host. "I'm afraid he just woke up from a sound sleep."

"I understand. Long transatlantic flights do the same thing to me." He'd said it with urbane sophistication, acting as if nothing was wrong, but she knew *he* knew there was plenty wrong with her son. "Let's gather your luggage."

They walked over to the carousel. "We have three cases. They're the navy ones with the red-and-white trim."

He reached for them, and they followed him outside past the other passengers to a black, four-door Jeep. He stowed the suitcases in the rear with what looked like effortless ease. To her consternation, the play of hard muscle across his back and shoulders drew her attention without her volition.

Andy just stood there without helping, causing Kit

more embarrassment. Their host spoke to him. "Do you prefer the front or backseat?"

"Back," he mumbled.

"I'll sit with you, honey." Kit opened the rear door and climbed in before Mr. Livingston had time to help. Andy got in next to her and pulled the door shut. Their host slid his powerful body behind the wheel of the Jeep, coughing again before they took off.

She glanced out her window so she wouldn't be tempted to stare at the way his black hair curled in tendrils against the bronzed skin of his neck. Since seeing him walk toward her in the terminal, she'd felt breathless, assuming it was because of the six thousand feet or more altitude after coming from sea level. But upon closer examination, she realized it was the stunning-looking male driving the Jeep who'd caused her lungs to constrict.

The farther away they got from the airport, the freer she felt, despite the tension emanating from both her son and the enigmatic male in front.

Maybe not enigmatic. That wasn't the word she was looking for. Still, something wasn't right. The cowboy's attitude wasn't as warm as the tone of his partner's letter that had touched her heart. She would have to wait until tonight after Andy had fallen asleep before she'd be able to apologize to their host about her son.

Perhaps coming here for the first week of September rather than anytime in August had put them out, though they hadn't seemed to mind when she'd asked if she could change the dates. After the generosity of these marines, changing the dates to please her in-laws had embarrassed her terribly. When she got the opportunity, she would explain what had happened.

Still troubled by her thoughts, she saw a jet climb into one of the bluest skies she'd ever seen. With the Grand Teton in the background, the sight was magnificent beyond words. She watched until the plane was a mere speck before she sighed with relief. They were really here, delivered to the small town of seven thousand people. It wasn't just a dream.

She'd been living for this moment. From now on their future plans rested solely with her.

Suddenly she felt their host's piercing glance on her through the rearview mirror. She could almost believe he was reading her mind. "If you're hungry, say the word and we can stop for a bite to eat in Jackson. Otherwise dinner is served from five to eight in the dining room of the main ranch house."

Anyone watching or listening would think he was being perfectly polite. He was, but behind his benign suggestion she still sensed he had reservations about her.

"I don't want to eat," Andy muttered to her before he turned and hunched against the door.

Kit didn't know if their host had heard him or not. Her son had completely forgotten his manners. "Thank you for asking, but we had a meal before we landed so we're fine until later."

"You don't even want something to drink?"

"No, thank you."

He turned onto the main highway. "We'll be at the ranch in fifteen minutes. There'll be drinks and snacks in your cabin."

"That sounds wonderful." In order to shut his compelling image from her vision, she closed her eyes, but another cough from him reminded her he was still there. He must be getting over a cold.

The first stage in her plan had been accomplished. She and Andy were far away from Maine and her in-laws. Unfortunately she hadn't expected a complication like Mr. Livingston. Despite the fact that he seemed to have reservations about her, she'd already become aware of him as a man, a disturbing one. This *awareness* hadn't happened to her since before her marriage to Winn. She didn't like it.

Chemistry had been responsible for their ill-advised union. Of course she could never regret Andy, who was the joy of her existence, but she was ten years older now and knew better than to get carried away a second time.

Kit's one purpose in life was to make a new life for her and Andy. Beyond that she couldn't think.

Chapter Two

Ross hadn't known what to expect while he'd been waiting for the Wentworths inside the terminal. He'd spotted a nice-looking dark blond boy of about nine or ten, dressed in shorts and a collared shirt, emerge from the doors. When Ross saw the mother directly behind him with her dark hair styled in tousled waves, he let out a low whistle.

She might be close to thirty at this point, but he did have to admit that in her recent widowhood, she could have passed as a top model for a fashion magazine. He liked her pleated white pants and the chic, short-sleeved khaki blouse that tucked in at the waist. She looked polished and sophisticated. Her sex appeal stood out a mile, catching the eye of most of the males in her sight, including his.

Damn if Charles Wentworth's daughter-in-law wasn't a knockout. Because of his own privileged background, he had a tendency to cast a jaded eye on women who thrived in a culture he'd found too shallow to tolerate.

The affluent society he'd grown up in was what had finally caused Ross to join the marines. A complete break from the life plan his father had mapped out for him was his only way out. He'd needed to get out, or his life wouldn't have been worth living. But his desire for a lifetime career in the military had come to an early end when he'd been discharged after six years of service because of his chronic cough.

Except to visit his parents after being released from Walter Reed Hospital in March, plus the monthly phone call home, he hadn't been near that world until today. By some strange quirk in the universe, it had fallen to him to be the personal host of this woman and her son.

Ross saw himself in Andy at that age and was haunted by it. The boy had grown up in the same kind of environment as Ross. Better than anyone else, he recognized a kid who could be corrupted by that kind of money and lifestyle. A child who was born to walk one path with no room for deviation.

But before he allowed past bitterness to overwhelm him, Ross needed to remember this mother and son had lost their husband and father. They'd come to the ranch at the guys' invitation and were his responsibility for the next week. Death came to every class of society, and they were still dealing with their grief.

Ross knew the usual tactics to win over a child the way Carson and Buck had done wouldn't work with Andy. It had been ingrained in this boy from infancy that he was superior to everyone else.

He came from an establishment fueled by money and power beyond most people's ability to imagine. Already he could see in the boy's eyes what an insufferable week he would have to spend in this back-of-beyond place. Ross would have to rely on his gut instinct to make any headway.

Once he turned onto the road leading into the ranch,

he pointed out the ranch managers' complex with homes and bunkhouses, the machinery and hay shed, the calving barn, the horse barn and corrals. Maybe the boy was listening, maybe not.

"Oh, Andy. Look how beautiful it is here with the river and the pines, honey. I'm reminded of a Disney cartoon where everything in nature is so perfect. Don't you think it looks like a peaceful little city immaculately laid out with the forest on one side and the Tetons standing guard on the other?"

To Ross's surprise her words echoed his own thoughts the first time he'd laid eyes on Carson's ranch.

Still no response from Andy, who looked and acted miserable.

"That's the main ranch house on the right. The cabins are farther on." Ross coughed again and kept driving until he came to the one reserved for them. As he pulled up to the front steps, she opened the door and got out to look around.

"We're surrounded with sage!" she exclaimed. "It's a heavenly smell."

"I agree," Ross muttered, confused by her reactions. Instead of a blasé view of everything topped off with a patronizing nod, she reminded him of a child who took delight in what she saw. If she was pretending to be something she wasn't, he'd be hard-pressed to prove it.

Andy climbed out his side of the Jeep. For the first time he looked at Ross. "How come you cough so much?"

"Andy!" she cried in embarrassment.

Contact at last. "It's all right, Mrs. Wentworth, a perfectly normal question. I'm not sick in the way you might think, Andy. My partners and I picked up a cough in Afghanistan from breathing bad air, the contaminants of war. You can't get it from being around me. Today it's a little worse because there's some smoke in the air from a forest fire. Smoke is our enemy. We always keep oxygen around to breathe in case it gets bad."

Andy studied him for a minute without saying anything. Mrs. Wentworth's exquisite sea-green eyes fringed with black lashes sought his. "Will you get better?" She sounded as if she really wanted to know.

"Maybe."

"In other words, you might never recover completely. I'm so sorry."

Ross shook his head, taken back by her seeming sincerity. "We're fine."

He transferred his gaze to Andy who was still eyeing him. "If anyone's sorry, we are for what happened to your father. He was a very brave marine who made himself a decoy under heavy fire and saved eight lives. I'm sure you've already been told the circumstances, but it bears repeating.

"Hold that knowledge to you, Andy. Not every person born on this earth has a dad like yours, who was willing to give his life for his friends and country. What he did was remarkable. None of us will ever forget. It's an honor to meet his son. If you'll let us, we'd love to show you a good time while you're here. Tomorrow I'll take you riding if you want."

If Ross didn't miss his guess, the boy's light gray eyes grew suspiciously bright before he looked down. Illness and death seemed to be the only two areas that had reached him so far. "You must be tired. I'll take in your luggage so you can get settled." He opened the back of the Jeep to get their bags.

"Come on, Andy. Let's help." She grabbed a case and handed it to him, then reached for one for herself. She kept surprising Ross. He took the other one and went up the steps first to open the cabin door.

"I love it!" she announced once they were inside. "Yellow and white are my favorite colors. This place is charming, Mr. Livingston. We're going to be so happy here, aren't we, Andy?"

Ross didn't expect him to answer, and the boy didn't disappoint him.

"There are two bedrooms." They followed him past the front room to the hallway. "The bathroom is behind that door. Which room would you like, Andy?" One room had a queen-size bed, the other contained twin beds.

"I guess that one." He meant the one on the right with the two beds.

"Good." Ross set down the case.

His mother joined them and lowered her case to the floor. "This cozy room will be perfect for both of us. We'll figure everything out later. Let's go check out the snacks."

Andy put the other suitcase down and gave his mother a startled glance before they all moved to the other room. "We're going to sleep in the same room?"

"Why not? We don't ever get to do it at home. I think it will be fun. We'll read stories to each other." She walked over to the table near the minifridge. "What's in these little pouches?"

"Pine nuts gathered on the ranch."

She smiled at Ross before putting a couple in her mouth. "Umm…nummy. Here, honey. Try some. Put out your hand." When Andy did her bidding, she poured a few in his palm, then she turned to Ross. "What about you?"

How could he say no? He didn't like admitting it, but she had a disarming way about her. "Thank you." He tossed back a few. "Just so you know, the maids come in daily to do housekeeping. If you need wash done, put it in the laundry bag hanging on the bathroom door and they'll return your clothes before evening."

"Talk about being pampered," she murmured. Just as he was thinking what a statement for her to make when you considered her background, her cell phone rang. She pulled it out of her pocket to check the caller ID. It wiped the smile from her face.

"Excuse me. I need to answer this." She clicked on and said hello. After a minute she said, "I planned to call you, but we just walked in our cabin with Mr. Livingston."

Another pause, then, "Yes. He's right here." She called to Andy, who was looking in the minifridge. "Your grandfather wants to talk to you."

"Do I have to?" he grumbled.

"I think you better."

Andy didn't look happy about it, but he walked over and reached for the phone. "Hello?" There was more silence before he said, "It's a nice ranch. I guess we'll be going riding. Mr. Livingston's going to take us." Whether that explanation was meant to satisfy his grandfather on some level or whether the idea of it actually sounded interesting to Andy, Ross didn't know yet.

"I'll be careful, but I've got to go now." Another pause. "I will." He hung up and whispered something to his mom.

Mother and son needed to be alone. Ross eyed them. "If you'll forgive me, I have an errand to run before dinner." Because of the smoke in the air he needed to take his medicine. "The dining room will be open in an hour. Shall I come by for you in the Jeep, or would you like to walk and meet me there? We'll discuss an itinerary for you while we eat."

"Oh, walk! Definitely." She escorted him to the door where he stepped out on the porch. "Thank you for everything, Mr. Livingston."

He detected a catch in her voice. His little talk to Andy would have affected her, too. She'd lost her husband, yet was trying to remain upbeat for her son. Ross admired that. Somehow her emotion had gotten under his skin. Facing her he said, "You're welcome, Mrs. Wentworth. Call me Ross."

"I'm Kit."

His brows lifted. "Is that your given name?"

"No. I was named Kathryn, but the grandmother who raised me after my parents died called me Kit and it stuck."

Ross liked it. She was the antithesis of the woman he'd been expecting once he'd known her background. Despite his initial misgivings, there were a dozen questions he wanted to ask, but this wasn't the time.

"I'm sorry about Andy," she said in a quiet voice.

"What do you mean?"

"He's been going through a bad time and knows better than to whisper in front of company. My father-in-law wants me to call him before I go to bed, that's all."

She hadn't owed him an explanation. "Don't worry about it. I'll see you later then." He climbed in the Jeep and took off without looking back.

After parking at the rear of the main ranch house, he entered the back door and strode swiftly down the hall to the stairs. He kept his medicine in his bathroom on the second floor.

"Hey, Ross?" At the sound of Willy's voice he swung around. "I saw you drive up when I was outside. You had a phone call that sounded important, if you know what I mean." He handed him a piece of paper with a phone number on it with a wink.

Ross was afraid he did. "Thanks." He took the stairs two at a time. When he reached the bedroom, he medicated himself and then lay down on the bed to find out who'd called him. It was Cindy. He needed to put an end to her hopes. She answered on the second ring.

"Hey, cowboy. Am I going to see you tonight?"

Cindy Lawrence had been a lot of fun, but the hungry kiss she'd given Ross last night had offered too much. He should have enjoyed it. The beautiful moonlit night, unusually warm, should have worked its magic. But if Ross hadn't known on the bar's dance floor that it would be the one and only hour he spent with her, he knew it now.

He'd made the mistake of asking the flirtatious waitress to do some line dancing with him because he hadn't wanted to go back to the ranch house last night until he was ready to crash. The upstairs of the house was too empty.

"Much as I'd like to drop in tonight, I won't be able to," he said, trying to let her down gently. "A new family of a fallen marine just arrived in Jackson this afternoon. They're our guests on the dude ranch for a while and I'm in charge. Thanks for the dancing. It was fun."

The eagerness faded from her voice. "In other words you're not coming back anytime soon."

No. The attraction simply wasn't there. He'd been with a lot of women since coming to Wyoming, but so far all his relationships had been fleeting. "You never know. It's a busy time on the ranch. See you around, Cindy."

Without wasting any more time, Ross phoned the oil company he'd been researching and arranged for a meeting on Monday out at the site. Then he hung up and set his watch alarm. The medicine was working on him, making him drowsy. He closed his eyes, realizing that when he was awakened in an hour, he'd be seeing Kit Wentworth again. The thought shouldn't matter to him, but somehow it did.

KIT WATCHED HER son go through the DVDs in the entertainment center. "Have you seen a movie you'd like to watch?" She got up from the kitchen table with a granola bar in her hand to look through the stack with him. The luxury of them being free like this had already gone to her head.

"How about *Up?* I know you haven't seen that one." The grandparents had his life so regimented, he rarely found time to watch TV or films.

"No. That's a dumb kid's movie."

"Dumb" had made up most of his vocabulary since

he'd found out they were coming to the ranch. Kit had hoped a new adventure might put him in a little happier mood. But it was possible the few friends his grand-parents allowed him to play with had said something negative about going to a dude ranch and he was only echoing their comments.

Kit's eyes took in the attractive surroundings. All the comforts of home were included in this small rect-angular log cabin: a table and minifridge, a couch and upholstered chairs in front of the fireplace. After liv-ing in the Wentworth mausoleum, she loved its rustic simplicity and the lightness of the decor.

Everything a person needed was right here, remind-ing her of the tiny home she'd once lived in with her grandmother in Point Judith, Rhode Island, where she'd been happy. It was there she'd met Winn.

The Blue Attic Book Shop where she'd worked had an outdoor display of discounted books. She'd been busy taking them all inside when Winn had walked by and begun chatting her up. He'd taken out one of the family yachts from Bar Harbor and had sailed down the coast with his friends. They'd pulled in at Point Judith to eat dinner. But he hadn't told her that information at the time and had only explained he and some buddies had been out sailing.

Kit had fallen hard for him and they'd married soon after. He'd taken his nineteen-year-old bride home to meet his family in Maine. They'd ended up living there in a controlling world of wealth and privilege she grew to detest.

It devastated her that the twenty-two-year-old man with the sun-kissed blond hair, smiling eyes and dark tan she'd fallen in love with had changed so much after they'd exchanged vows. Once under his parents' thumb, nothing she'd done had been right. The way she'd looked and behaved hadn't satisfied him.

In an effort to please him, she'd transformed herself into the woman he'd seemed to want, a style maven like his mother Florence, or his two older married sisters, Corinne and Sybil, who considered themselves the original aristocrats of Bar Harbor. Still, Kit had never fit in.

After Andy had been born, Winn hadn't shown as much interest in her except when they'd gone to the family's various exclusive clubs where they'd been seen in public. Then it had all been show. They'd grown so far apart, she'd begged for them to get a home of their own. His sisters and their husbands had their own homes. But Winn had told her there was no reason for them to move when they were living in the mansion and offered every luxury.

The years had gone by—empty years for her. Winn's long deployments in the military had driven them further apart. When she'd found the courage to tell him she wanted a divorce, he'd told her the Wentworths didn't divorce. If she filed, she'd lose Andy because he wouldn't let her take him anywhere.

As a member of the family now, she had the responsibility of carrying on as his wife and widow. The man she'd married had disappeared, never to return. The best part of him, the part she preferred to remember, lived in Andy.

But her son's life had been strung out with long periods of waiting for his father to come home on leave. Even when he came, they hadn't spent enough quality time together because his parents had had other plans for him. For the long months in between visits, Andy had been expected to mind his grandparents who ruled his life.

She'd cried herself to sleep at night for years worrying about her darling son. Though he would be good-looking like Winn when he was grown, it wouldn't be long before he turned into a clone of his rigid grandfather.

Kit had kept her demons hidden from Andy the best she could, but now that they were here, she would have the conversation with him she'd been waiting for since Winn's death. Maybe tomorrow or the next day when he'd had a good sleep and was more relaxed.

She went in the bedroom to open one of the suitcases. After gathering up some items, she put them on the bedside table in their room. Besides a pocket radio, there was a photograph of Winn and another of her grandmother. She carried some treasured books to the living room. Kit planned to read aloud to Andy if he'd let her.

Once that was done, she went to the bathroom to brush her hair. When she came out she said, "I don't know about you, but I'm starving. Let's walk to the ranch house." He mumbled something and went out the door. She followed with the cabin card key Mr. Livingston had left on the table and made sure the place was locked before starting off.

The magnificent Tetons were right there in her vision, stunning her with their beauty. They headed for the fabulous ranch house in the distance. She was reminded of one like it on the cover of one of her favorite

Louis L'Amour Western novels. That was among the books she'd packed for this trip.

Kit had loved books in her early teens and had grown into a voracious reader. Her grandmother had gotten her hooked on all kinds of fiction, especially Westerns. One of the rooms in the house she'd rented had been turned into a virtual library.

After her grandmother died, Kit had kept a few favorites and donated the rest to the bookshop where she'd worked. The owner had allowed her to establish a lending library with the understanding that Kit would take the collection back when she had her own place. Winn didn't want them at the mansion. It almost killed her when last year she'd found out the shop had been sold and turned into a restaurant. All those precious books were gone....

Just seeing the ranch house with the pines clustered around the side brought back fond memories for the girl who'd grown up on the cape of Point Judith with her sweet grandmother and her books. But besides horses, this Western scene included the Jeep and all sorts of modern vehicles that must have belonged to the staff.

They followed some other guests inside and entered a large foyer. The mid-twenties guy behind the front desk flashed her a friendly smile loaded with a lot of male interest, the flattering kind. "Hi! Can I help you?"

"Yes. I'm Kit Wentworth, and this is my son, Andy. Mr. Livingston told us to meet him here for dinner."

His eyes widened. "You're our special guests from Maine?"

She smiled. "That's right."

"Welcome to the ranch. Here's another card key so you can both have access to your cabin."

"Thank you." She handed it to Andy, who looked surprised before putting it in the pocket of his shorts. "We're very grateful to have been invited."

"I guess you haven't had the grand tour."

"Not yet."

"The dining room's right through the great room across the foyer. There's a games room at the other end, and beyond the doors you'll come to a swimming pool with a lifeguard on duty. Go ahead and look around. I'm sure he'll be along shortly."

"Thanks so much."

They walked through the next room past the massive fireplace and into the dining room filled with the regular dude ranch guests, many in Western gear. One of the first things on her list was to buy them some fun cowboy stuff so they'd fit in around here.

Andy looked up. "They've got wagon wheels for lights!"

Her gaze went to the vaulted ceiling. "These are the kind of chandeliers I prefer any day. Pretty cool, don't you think?" Red-and-white checkered cloths covered the tables. She liked the yellow-and-white daisy centerpieces that reminded her of their cabin's colors.

"I guess." Though he played it down, the fact that he'd noticed gave her hope he was starting to thaw a little at having to be here.

She found them an empty table over on one side of the room. They each took a menu and studied it. "What do you think you want, honey?"

"A hamburger?" Hamburgers weren't on the menu at

the Wentworth mansion. She had come to dread their five-course meals where the inevitable question-and-answer period lasted at least an hour. She knew Andy hated the length of time they had to stay at the table.

"That sounds good to me, too, with lots of French fries. Shall we splurge and get chocolate malts for dessert?"

"Can we?"

Why not? This was a night of celebration. "We can have anything we want here." She eyed him with concern. "This dude ranch isn't turning out to be such a bad place. Right?"

He looked away without answering, but when the friendly waitress came over, he gave her his order instead of just sitting there silently. This was the Andy she needed to see come back.

"How are you feeling by now? I know that medicine made you feel kind of strange."

"I hate the way it makes me so sleepy."

"I know, but at least it kept you from throwing up."

Before long the waitress returned with their food. He swallowed his in no time. It was surprising to her, considering he hadn't shown much appetite on the cruise. She was only halfway through her meal but could tell he was already restless. Who wouldn't be after their long flights?

"While I finish eating, why don't you go have a look around? The man at the desk mentioned a games room and swimming pool."

"You mean you'll let me?"

His grandparents had kept him on a short leash. "Sure."

He eyed her in surprise. "Thanks." Kit hadn't heard that word from her son in a long, long time.

Kit watched him dart away with more energy than she'd noticed in ages. Relieved to see him behave like a normal boy for a few minutes, she ate some more French fries and kept an eye out for her host. Just when she decided something must have detained him, she saw him walk through the door from the kitchen.

His dark brown gaze panned the room. The male charisma oozing from him took her breath. Judging by the female guests in the room, they had the same reaction. Though there were quite a few men seated around, none of them affected her like Ross Livingston. Marine or cowboy, he seemed a breed apart.

He still hadn't seen her and started walking through the tables. As he drew closer, she called to him. His head turned in her direction. The second their eyes met, it grew into one of those moments when the world stood still for her. It was happening again. That awareness...

Ross moved toward her. Without his cowboy hat, his head of wavy black hair and arresting male features pretty well dazed her. She wondered who the lucky woman was who'd captured this attractive man's attention. There had to a woman, maybe a wife, even if he didn't wear a ring, and she would be exceptional.

"I'm sorry I was too late to eat with you. Business detained me." He sounded disappointed.

"Please don't apologize for anything." The pulse in her throat was throbbing so hard, she couldn't finish the last bites of her meal.

"Where's Andy?"

"When he was through eating, he went out exploring. I'm almost done and was about to look for him."

"Then let's go together."

"What about your dinner?"

"I had a snack already and will eat later."

Ross walked her out into the warm air. The sun wouldn't be going down for a while. There were half a dozen people in the pool. He nodded to the lifeguard.

"Hey, Uncle Ross—over here!"

A dripping wet Johnny Lundgren stood by the diving board talking nonstop to none other than their latest guest. Johnny was a little short for his age. Andy seemed to be tall for a nine-year-old. But the difference in height and age didn't mean a thing to Johnny. He was the friendliest kid on the planet. Ross smiled at the scene.

"That's Carson Lundgren's adopted son talking Andy's ear off," he said in an aside to Kit. "He's already adopted me and Buck as his uncles."

"How sweet," she murmured with genuine tenderness. She'd just described Carson's son. They walked to the end of the pool.

"Johnny? This is Andy's mom, Kit. They're from Maine."

"Hi, Johnny," she said with warmth.

"Hi! I just asked Andy if he wants to come riding with me and Jenny in the morning. He's never ridden on a pony before."

"I think that sounds fun, but we don't know what Ross has planned for us yet."

Johnny turned to Andy. "He'll probably take you

fishing, but I think riding is more fun. Do you want to get in the pool and swim with me?"

If anyone could make a dent in Andy's armor, it was Johnny, who'd just given Ross an opening he'd take. "Why don't we all swim? I'll go inside and put on my suit. It's the perfect temperature out here."

"Hooray!" Johnny cried in excitement.

Andy turned to his mother. In a quiet voice he said, "I don't want to."

"Then you don't have to, but after sitting on a plane for hours, I feel like a swim. I'm going to run to our cabin for my suit."

"Mom—"

"I'll be right back, honey."

Ross could see and feel Andy's frustration as she disappeared. The fact that she'd taken Ross up on the idea meant she wasn't about to coddle her son. Again he gave her marks for expecting Andy to deal with this new situation despite his unhappiness.

"Don't you guys have fun without me!" he said to the two of them.

Johnny laughed. "You're funny, Uncle Ross."

No sound came out of Andy. He just looked at him in bewilderment before Ross took off. At least that was a change from the scowl he'd worn during the drive from the airport.

Ross reached his room and changed into his black trunks. After grabbing a towel, he hurried back down and belly flopped next to Johnny on purpose, causing him to laugh. Ross noticed Andy sitting in a deck chair by himself.

"Come on, Johnny. Let's go talk to him." As he

hoisted him on his shoulders, he saw Kit come out on the patio carrying a rolled-up towel.

"Hi, everybody!" In seconds she removed her wrap. Ross's breath caught to see her shapely body clad in a light blue bikini dive into the deep end of the pool from the side. When she surfaced, she swam over to her son. "I brought your suit in the towel. If you change your mind, use the cabana."

When he didn't respond, Ross said, "We're going to play sharks and minnows."

Johnny's head jerked around. "Hey—I haven't played that game before."

"It's a new one I've been waiting to teach you. I'm the shark and you guys are the minnows. I'll be at the end of the pool. You and Kit get up on the side of the deck. I'll call out, sharks and minnows, one two three, fishies, fishies swim to me. That's when you'll dive in and swim to the other side. If I don't catch you, then you'll be the shark for the next round. If I do, then you'll stay a minnow."

Johnny giggled. "That sounds silly."

He grinned. "You think? Just wait until I come after you." His gaze swerved to Kit who'd climbed up on the deck ready to play. Ross had a devil of a time concentrating when he couldn't take his eyes off her.

"Come on, Johnny. Let's see if we can beat this big shark at his own game." The way she'd said it heightened Ross's anticipation.

"Yeah!" Johnny got out of the water and walked over by her.

"Sharks and minnows—" Ross called out after coughing. The game was on. They must have played six rounds, but Ross beat them every time. Both she and Johnny came up laughing and spurting.

"How come you guys can't catch me?" Ross baited them. "I thought you said this was a silly game, Johnny."

Out of the corner of his eye he saw Andy, who'd come out of the cabana in his suit and was watching. *Well, what do you know.* Nothing like a little healthy competition.

"Come on, Andy," Johnny shouted when he saw him. "Help us win!"

Once again they lined up along the side, but this time Andy had joined them. "Sharks and minnows—" Ross called out. There was plenty of splashing as everyone dived into the pool. Ross went after the other two first so he would barely miss tagging Andy.

"Hey—now Andy's a shark!"

"He sure is, Johnny." Ross smiled at Kit's son. "How did you learn to swim so fast?"

"I don't know."

"You're good!" Ross climbed up next to Johnny and Kit. She thanked him with her eyes. While he was still staring into them Andy shouted, "Sharks and minnows—" The boy was a quick study.

By Ross losing his concentration, Andy tagged him and Kit with no problem. That made Johnny the winner.

"Bravo!" another voice called out.

"Mom!" Johnny cried. Tracy had just come out to the pool. "Uncle Ross taught us a new game and I won this time! Put your suit on and get in."

"Honey, it's late. The pool is closed now. Time to get out."

"Oh, heck."

"Your mom's right, Johnny. But there's always tomorrow."

He scrambled out of the pool to his mother who wrapped him in a towel. After kissing him, she said, "It looks like we have some new guests."

"Yup. That's Andy and his mom, Kit. They're from Maine."

Ross took over. "Kit Wentworth? Meet Carson's wife, Tracy."

"It's so nice to meet you, Mrs. Lundgren. Andy and I are thrilled to be here."

"We've all been looking forward to your arrival, haven't we, Johnny."

"Yeah. Please, will you come riding with us in the morning?"

Andy shrugged. "I guess."

"Goody! We'll let you pick out one of the ponies to ride, but I think you'll like Raindrop. She's a dappled gray. You're older than we are and she's a little bigger than the others. She likes apple nuggets for a treat."

Ross chuckled. "She does love those."

Kit smiled. "I can't wait to see her. With that settled, we'd better get out of the pool and change. After our long flight we're about ready for bed and will see all of you tomorrow. Come on, Andy."

"Bye, Andy. See ya later." Johnny walked away with his mother.

"Bye."

Ross turned to his guests. "I'll meet you in the foyer in five minutes to drive you back to the cabin."

"We'll hurry," she assured him.

Before long the three of them met by the front desk

where there were a few guests checking in. Ross was pleased to see their normal dude ranch business was continuing to grow.

Willy looked up. "Hey, Ross—I see they found you." But his eyes were so focused on Kit, Ross would have laughed if the situation weren't so precarious. Her dark hair still had natural curl when it was damp. She looked good. Too good. He had to remember they were honoring her husband's memory.

"We did," Kit spoke up. She appeared oblivious to Willy's gawking. "Thank you."

Ross walked them through the front door to the parking area on the side of the ranch house. "We'll go in the truck." He opened the rear passenger door for them, and they climbed inside.

Once on their way, he heard Andy talking to his mother in the back. "That Johnny's funny."

"He's very cute. I think it will be fun to go riding with him."

"Ponies are for babies."

"Johnny didn't look like a baby to me."

Good for Kit.

When they reached the cabin, Ross shut off the engine and turned in the seat to expand on her comment. "When you're seven, a pony is a lot easier to handle. Johnny's adoptive father, Carson, is a champion rodeo rider who owns this ranch. He got him started on Goldie in June. You should see how he rides already."

Ross could hear the boy mulling everything over in his mind. "What happened to his real father?"

Andy didn't miss much. "He was a brave marine like your dad who died in the war. Like you, we invited him and his mom to come to the ranch for a week. They ended up staying, and now they're married."

"How wonderful for them," Kit murmured.

Ross agreed, but the boy had gone quiet. Figuring he'd said enough for now, he climbed down from the truck and opened the rear door for Kit. They both got out the same side. Kit pulled the key card from her pocket to unlock the cabin door, drawing his gaze to the shape of womanly hips below her waist. As for the curves above…it was no wonder Willy couldn't keep his eyes to himself.

She turned to him. "Good night. Thank you for everything."

To his surprise he didn't want to leave. "I'll come by for you at eight in the morning, and we'll have breakfast together before planning our day. Good night, you two."

Ross got in the truck and took off for the ranch house. Before heading upstairs he made a detour to the kitchen for a sandwich and bumped into Buck stealing a donut on his way to bed.

These days his friend wore a continual smile. That's what being deeply in love did for you.

"Hey—" He nudged Ross, then coughed. "Willy just told me about Mrs. Wentworth and her son. Apparently she's one gorgeous babe. His words, I swear."

"If you like brunettes."

"You don't?"

"I never said that." The last word came out on a cough.

He studied him. "What's she like? Don't tell me she's *nice*."

Ross bit into his ham sandwich. "What if she is?"

Buck chuckled. "And her son?"

"He's got problems."

"But nothing you can't handle."

"I don't know. It's early days yet." The conversation Andy had had with his grandfather earlier still puzzled him. Until the phone call, the boy hadn't said two words. Then he'd switched to talking mode, but only after he'd been urged by his mother to come to the phone. Ross didn't know what to make of the tension.

"Are you all right?"

"Ask me in a week." Ross couldn't take more of the interrogation. He finished off his sandwich, knowing sleep wouldn't come for a while. "Good night."

The guys had warned Ross that lightning could strike three times in the same place, and they had the documented video to prove it. He'd laughed off their teasing, but for some reason he wasn't laughing now.

Chapter Three

After washing and blow drying her hair, Kit got ready
for bed. When she peeked in their bedroom, she discovered that Andy had fallen asleep. Considering their long
day, it didn't surprise her. Without waiting another minute, she went into the living room to phone her in-laws.

"Hello, Florence? Andy told me you wanted me to
call before we went to bed."

"We expected to hear from you before now."

"I'm sorry, but we swam until late with the owner's
son, Johnny Lundgren. He's two years younger than
Andy, but a real joy and a lot of fun."

Ross's suggestion that they all swim had turned out
to be inspirational. By dreaming up that little competition, Ross had nudged Andy out of his mood. Andy
hadn't been able to resist joining in and had won a
round. The praise their host had given him had made a
subtle difference in her son, increasing his confidence.
Kit could have hugged Ross for it.

"Where's Andy?" Charles spoke up from another
extension.

"In bed, sound asleep."

"What are your plans for tomorrow?"

She frowned. "I don't know yet. Probably riding. Why?"

"I'm concerned about Andy. The weather can change on a dime out there. I don't want to hear you took my grandson up on the Grand Teton with all those lightning strikes. You shouldn't have gone to Wyoming."

He's my *son, Charles,* she wanted to shout at him. But she understood that after losing Winn, her in-laws were fearful of other losses. Instead she said, "There are too many other activities planned right here on the ranch for you to worry about that. It's supposed to be warm weather the whole time while we're here. We're going to concentrate on riding horses and fly-fishing on the Snake. This is a glorious place." Like a piece of heaven.

"I was there years ago. The Snake River can be dangerous."

She took a deep breath. "Charles? I promise our hosts aren't going to allow us to do any activity where we can get hurt. They're trying to make this an exciting adventure for Andy." Kit had already been given proof of that at the pool with Ross.

"But you're there without Winn."

"Andy and I have each other, Florence. Now if you'll forgive me, I'm exhausted and need to get to bed. It's late for you, too."

"We'll talk tomorrow," Charles announced in his imperious voice.

Oh, she knew that. Twice a day and every night like clockwork. "I'll have Andy call you after our ride tomorrow. He'll have lots to tell you, I'm sure. Good night."

She hung up and hurried to bed. Moonlight kept the

cabin room from being totally dark. Sleeping in the same room with her son was a brand-new experience. When Winn had been home, he'd never allowed Andy to get in bed with them, even when he was a small child.

And when he'd been away, he'd insisted Andy stay in his own bedroom on the next floor, and his parents had enforced his rule. She'd slept by him a few times over the years when he'd been sick and needed comfort, but this was different. While they were on vacation, she relished this time alone with him so they could really talk.

Kit turned on her side to face him. As she drifted off, her mind relived those moments in the swimming pool with Ross. She wished she didn't find him so appealing. She hadn't come here with the idea of meeting a man. Anything but.

Unfortunately, Ross was the first person on her mind when she woke up the next morning. The knowledge that he'd be coming for them in a few minutes gave her stomach flutters.

Andy had already gotten out of bed and was watching TV. She called to him to come and get ready.

"How did you sleep?"

"Good."

"Are you hungry?"

"Yeah."

She mulled over his answers while they put on their shoes. "Good" and "yeah" were signs his mood had improved. If only he would stay this way...

"Mom? Did you call Grandfather last night?"

He'd been her little worrier for years. "I did, but let me ask you something. What would you think if I hadn't phoned him?"

Andy swung his head toward her. She saw that nervous look he often got. "You know," he muttered.

She'd finished doing her hair and put the brush down. "You mean he'd get mad. You can say it, honey."

His eyes slid away.

"It's not much fun to be around someone grumpy, is it?"

He didn't respond.

"He and your grandmother get mad at me, too." She applied some lipstick.

"I know."

Her son understood a lot, but she still had to probe to get at the truth of how he truly felt about his life.

"That's why it's nice you and I can be on vacation by ourselves. We all need a break, don't you think?"

His faint nod gave her the sign she'd been hoping for, but they both heard a horn honk out front. She would have to continue this conversation with him later.

"Let's go." She put the card key in her pocket. With a happier heart, she followed him out the door into another day filled with sunshine, sage and Ross Livingston as she lived and breathed. He'd dressed in a brown-and-white plaid Western shirt and a pair of jeans that molded powerful thighs.

She felt his eyes on her as they filed out to the truck. Then they flicked to her son.

"Hey, Andy—how's it going?"

"Good."

"If you want, hop up in the back of the truck. You can ride on one of those bales of hay."

"Sure." Kit watched him heave himself up without Ross trying to help. Their host was the opposite of Charles who micromanaged him every second of his life.

"One of these days Johnny will be able to do that," he confided to Andy.

Thank you, Ross. His way with Andy, combined with his goodness, wrapped itself around Kit's insides, warming her through to the empty spaces in her heart.

"On the way to breakfast we'll pick up Johnny. Between him and Buck's new stepdaughter, Jenny, you'll be among friends. I know they're two years younger than you, but they'll like being with you. You've lived in Maine and know a lot of neat stuff they don't. And one more thing. They're fun."

"Johnny makes me laugh."

"He makes me laugh, too."

Keep this up, Ross. You're a genius.

His grin was infectious. Kit felt it radiate until her toenails curled. When Ross turned around, she was caught staring at him. "What about you? You want the joy of sitting on a hay bale, as well?"

She chuckled. He could have no idea what she was feeling at the moment, but now wasn't the time to try and put it into words. "I think I'll ride in the cab." In a minute she climbed in the passenger side of the truck and shut the door. Once settled, she turned to him, trying not to be distracted by his male charisma.

While they drove, she said, "When I accepted the invitation to come to the ranch, I didn't expect to receive such personalized service. Since you mentioned your partners' children, I assume you're married, too. I don't want any of you to feel you have to give us your attention round the clock."

"This is my job. But to clear up any misunderstanding, I'm still single."

Her heart fluttered in her chest. "Even so, you must have other calls on your time."

"That's true."

He might not be married, but he'd just let her know he had his own love life. While she was immersed in contemplating that fact, she barely noticed they'd driven up in front of a fabulous glass and wood house beyond some pines. It overlooked the Snake River, and behind it she saw the majesty of the Grant Teton. The sight never ceased to thrill her.

He pulled to a stop. "I'll see if Johnny wants to come and have breakfast with us." Ross levered himself from the driver's seat with that swift male grace particular to him. He called to Andy who jumped down from the back of the truck, and the two of them walked through the grass to the front porch.

Tracy, dressed in a robe, opened the door. A cute black-and-white Boston terrier ran circles around Ross and Andy, causing laughter before Tracy invited them in.

Several minutes later they came back out with Johnny, who was talking a blue streak. He'd dressed in a black cowboy hat and cowboy boots. Kit thought she'd never seen a cuter sight in her life. The dog followed him to the truck and then hurried into the house again.

While Andy climbed in the back, Ross helped Johnny, then he joined her in the cab, pinning her with his dark brown gaze. "Tracy wanted to say hi but it will have to be later, after she's dressed. Carson has already left to do chores." He backed the truck around, and they headed for the ranch house.

"That little boy is adorable."

"You have a great son, too, but it's clear he's passed the adorable stage."

She couldn't hold back a chuckle. "You can say that again. But I heard him laugh a second ago. Yesterday I feared that sound had become extinct."

"After losing his father, I'm not surprised. We'll see what we can do to get him to do it more often."

Kit decided that if anyone could perform that miracle, Ross could. She marveled over his dedication. There wasn't anything about him she didn't like…and the thought made her increasingly worried.

In a few minutes they reached the side parking of the ranch house. She got out so he wouldn't walk around to help her. Andy jumped down. Johnny tried to copy him, but Ross, ever alert, was there to make sure he didn't hurt himself. "Come on, everybody. Let's find a table and chow down."

BUCK WAVED TO their group from one of the tables. The dining room was full of guests, great news for business. "Over here. Jenny and I have been waiting for you guys."

Ross could always count on his partners and introduced Andy to the two of them before they sat down. "Buck Summerhayes? Jenny Forrester? Meet Andy and his mother, Kit Wentworth. They've come all the way from Bar Harbor, Maine, to be our guests."

"Andy and I are very pleased to meet all of you. Thank you for making us feel so welcome. We're the luckiest people in the world to have been invited here." When she smiled like that, she lit up the place.

Jenny looked up. She was a charming seven-year-old blonde girl who'd grow up to be as beautiful as her grandmother, Alex, one day. This morning she was wearing her white cowboy hat, ready to ride.

She looked at Andy with curiosity. "Did you fly here?"

"Yes."

"Did you like it?"

"No. I got airsick and had to take medicine."

"I got sick when I flew here, too. There was a big storm."

"I didn't get sick," Johnny piped up, "but it was sure scary. I thought we were going to crash."

Ross handed Andy a menu. "What do you like for breakfast?"

"I don't like breakfast that much."

"What do you eat?" Johnny asked. Now that they were seated, Ross could count on Carson's son to carry the conversation from here on out. "I like Froot Loops."

"I've never had those."

"How come?"

"We always have to eat poached eggs and toast. My grandmother makes me eat grapefruit so I won't get fat."

"Ew!" the two children said in a collective voice.

Jenny looked at Andy. "Does your grandmother live with you?"

"We live with both my grandparents."

Andy had just dropped a bombshell on Ross. Until this second he didn't know Kit and her son lived in the famous Wentworth mansion, too. Had this been since her husband's death? He remembered Andy's surprise when Kit had told him they would sleep in the same bedroom at the cabin.

"After my mommy died, I lived with my nana, but she lets me eat what I want."

Johnny made a face. "If my mom gave me grapefruit, I'd feed it to Blackie."

Ross's chuckle brought on a cough. "I don't think your dog would like it either."

Jenny's blue eyes had widened. "You've never had cereal?"

"We had oatmeal sometimes," Kit explained, "but not many choices for uncooked cereal."

"That's *mean*."

"That's really mean," Johnny concurred.

Ross thought he was going to crack up with laughter and noticed Kit was trying hard not to laugh, too.

"Do you want to try Boo Berry?" Jenny asked. "It's my favorite."

"Okay."

"It makes your teeth blue," Johnny informed him. "Will your mom get mad if you eat it?"

"Of course I won't," Kit supplied with spirit. "When I lived with my grandmother, we ate a lot of cereal."

Andy stared at his mother in surprise. "You did?"

"Yes. Lucky Charms were my favorite, along with eggs and fruit. Maybe Boo Berry will turn out to be yours."

As Buck flashed Ross a private glance that sent a message of masculine approval, the waitress came over to take their orders. He heard Kit tell Andy that since they were on vacation, he could get whatever he wanted.

After listening to the other kids, her son asked for Boo Berry and hot chocolate. Pure sugar. What else?

"When does your school start?"

The question caught Kit's attention. "Since we're here on this wonderful trip, we're not worrying about that yet, Johnny."

"You're lucky. We have Back To School Night on Wednesday."

Jenny nodded. "Our classes start on Thursday. I hope our teacher isn't mean."

Buck grinned. "What's all this *mean* business, Red?" It was his nickname for her because she loved the color red so much. "When I was in school, I liked my teachers."

"All of them?"

"Well, maybe one or two of them weren't exactly my favorite people."

Johnny giggled.

"My grandparents are sending me away to a private school," Andy interjected.

Both children stared at him in shock. "Away from your mom?" Jenny asked.

He nodded.

Johnny put his spoon down. "How come?"

Kit wiped her mouth with the napkin. "Over the years all boys in the Wentworth family are sent to a special private boarding school when they turn nine. They can only come home twice a month if they've been good students."

"Boy, am I glad I'm not you!"

"Me, too," Jenny exclaimed. "My father and mother

died. If I had to go to a school away from my nana, I'd
run away."

Ross groaned inside, remembering his own painful years when he'd been sent away to the same kind
of school.

At this point the waitress brought their food, and they
tucked in. Ross looked at Kit, who'd gone quiet and was
busy eating. When he got her alone he'd find out what
was bothering her. In the meantime he had an idea to
change the direction of the conversation.

"Before we saddle up, we need to drive into town
and get some cowboy hats and boots for Kit and Andy."

"Goody!" Johnny enthused. "I need some more caps
for my mustang. I've been saving up my allowance."

"I'm going to buy some more caps, too," Jenny
chimed in.

"Let's get Andy a mustang, Uncle Ross."

"Only if he wants one."

Kit's son looked at Ross. "What's a mustang?"

"A cap gun."

"Yeah. Uncle Ross will be the bad guy and we'll go
hunting for him." Johnny was one in a million. "Do
you like cap guns?"

"I've never had one."

"Neither did I until my dad got me one at the Boot
Corral. They don't have them in Cleveland. That's
where my grandparents live."

Ross noticed a shadowed expression on Andy's face
and wondered what had put it there.

"I have my nana right here."

"We sure do, sweetheart." Buck hugged Jenny.

To Ross, the children's conversation had been like a

cacophony of enjoyable music until he'd looked at Kit's son; then the music had stopped.

He pushed himself away from the table and got to his feet. "If everyone's finished eating, let's leave for town. The sooner we get the shopping done, the sooner we can go riding. We'll take the van." Ross shot Buck a glance. "I'll look after Jenny."

His friend nodded. "I'll tell Alex. She's going to be at the front desk this morning. That'll give me time to finish installing that new cabinet in the office."

The kids ran out of the ranch house to the parking area and piled in the dark green van with the Teton Valley Dude Ranch Logo. Andy followed with his mother, who climbed in the front seat. He got in back with Johnny and Jenny.

"Everybody buckle up."

"You always say that."

He eyed Johnny through the rearview mirror. "And I always will."

"There's sure a lot of cars," Jenny observed as they turned onto the highway.

"That's because it's the Labor Day weekend."

"I completely forgot about that," Kit exclaimed. "No wonder the plane was full."

Ross coughed. "A lot of families want to come and have fun before school starts. All our cabins are full." So were the shops in town. Normally the Boot Corral wasn't crowded this early in the day.

The kids looked at all the cowboy hats. "What color do you want, Andy?"

"I don't know."

While the kids tried to talk him into hats like theirs,

Ross walked over to him. "My partners and I have seen pictures of your dad. You look a lot like him and should have a distinctive hat that suits your coloring. See anything that appeals to you?"

After a minute of looking he said, "Maybe that one."

"You mean this brown Stetson?" He nodded. Ross picked it up. "This is a Seminole Gus Buffalo felt cowboy hat."

His gray eyes rounded. "Buffalo?"

"Genuine buffalo felt. Nice, huh? I like the sloped pinch-front crown. Want to try it on for size?"

"I guess." Andy put it on his head and looked in the mirror.

Ross lowered the brim a little for him. "With those gray eyes you have that make-my-day kind of look. I'd say you look like a real cowboy." He glanced at Kit. "What do you say, Mom?" His question ended with a cough.

She studied her son with pride. "It transforms you, honey."

The kids walked over. Jenny eyed him. "It makes you look taller and different."

"That's the whole idea," Ross told her.

"Thanks." Andy glanced at his mother. "You should get a hat, too."

"You think?"

Johnny hurried over to her. "Get a black one like mine and Hoppy's."

Her gaze met Ross's before she smiled. "You mean Hopalong Cassidy?"

"Yeah. I love him! So does my dad!"

"What a great idea! I happen to love him, too."

"How come?"

"Because I've read a lot of cowboy books in my life and I have a collection of all the books about Hopalong."

Kit didn't know it yet, but she'd just made Johnny's day and had given Ross a heart attack with that smile. Hopalong had been a fictitious cowboy of the Old West depicted in film whom Carson had loved. It had captured Johnny's imagination.

"Why don't you pick it out for me, Johnny?"

"Okay." He walked back and forth inspecting all of them. "I like this one."

Jenny smiled at her. "Put it on!"

"Go on, Mom."

Ross watched as another transformation occurred. A good-looking woman in a cowboy hat had an allure you couldn't beat. "You and Andy will have to get boots that match your hats."

Once they were fitted, they decided to wear their cowboy boots and hats out of the store and carry their regular shoes in a bag to take home.

After the kids bought more ammo with their allowance money, Ross insisted on paying for everything else and threw in a couple of cap guns and ammo for him and Andy. Johnny had designated him the bad guy, so why not play the part all the way?

"Compliments of the ranch," he told Kit when she protested.

Beneath the rim of her black hat, her eyes went a darker green, if that was at all possible. "Thank you for everything." He knew what she was really saying. In his grief Andy might think a lot of things were dumb, but he hadn't fought getting himself a hat. Progress, inch by inch.

"We aim to please." He had trouble dragging his gaze away before turning to the kids. "I think we're ready to leave."

"Hooray! Daddy will be waiting for us at the stable." Johnny was the first one out the door to the van. Ross drove them back to Carson's house so he could get his cap gun, then they continued on to the ranch house. Jenny ran inside to get her gun while everyone got out of the van.

"Everyone in the truck for the ride over!"

Andy gave Johnny a nudge into the back before getting in himself. Good for him. Ross put the sack of shoes in back with the kids. Once he'd lifted Jenny inside, he shoved his hat on and they headed for the stable. Their little group was starting to mesh.

Kit watched them through the back window. "They're loading up like they're preparing to go to war, and Andy's doing it right along with them. When we flew in yesterday, I couldn't have imagined it. They all look so cute in their hats and boots. Can you see them?"

He could, but he preferred focusing on her. "Your son looks great in that Stetson."

She flicked him a glance. "You keep saying and doing the right things. You and your partners had to have been inspired to carry out this program."

"We needed to do something to justify our existence."

"I'm glad it's working out so well for you," she said in a husky voice. "Too bad there's no magic wand to take away your cough. It isn't fair."

"Is anything?"

Kit bowed her head. "No, but you handle it without complaint. You men are role models for the rest of us."

"Don't we wish."

The sound of the childrens' laughter accompanied them all the way to the stable.

Chapter Four

Kit drank in the beauty of the surroundings, needing to pinch herself as a reminder that this pine-studded paradise was real. They'd only been here since yesterday, yet already she needed to tamp down her euphoria or she might jump out of her skin.

Some of the other dude ranch guests were already saddled and had started out on a trail leading away from the corral. Her host pulled to a stop near the barn and helped Jenny down from the back. The boys got out, and the children disappeared inside with him.

Kit followed. She watched with sheer feminine pleasure as he strode toward the barn on those long powerful legs. In cowboy boots he was probably six foot four of lean, hard muscle. The usual adjectives didn't begin to describe Ross's effect on her senses or her psyche.

Once inside he flashed her a comprehensive glance. "Kit Wentworth, this is Bert Rawlins, who's been running the stable for years. He takes care of everything around here."

She put out her hand to shake the seasoned cowboy's hand. "It's a pleasure to meet you."

"Welcome to the ranch. Have you done any riding?"

"Some."

"Then let's get you up on Daisy. She's a gentle mare, but she has spirit." He brought out a tan horse from one of the stalls and saddled her.

Ross took over and walked her outside to the corral to help Kit mount. "Are you all right up there?"

If he only knew. She gripped the reins. "I'm fine, thank you."

"I'll go help Carson with the kids. He has a way with them and will make sure your son is perfectly safe on Raindrop."

"I know that." His letter had conveyed an almost spiritual essence that was very touching. If the owner of the ranch and former rodeo champion had half of Ross's heroic qualities, she could believe anything about these remarkable retired marines.

In another minute all three children on ponies rode out of the barn in their riding gear. The ponies were as beautiful and unique as their riders. Kit reached for her cell phone to take a picture, but realized she must have forgotten to bring it with her.

"Mom—" Andy had finally noticed her on Daisy near the corral fencing.

"Hi, honey! Just look at you guys! I bet it's fun to be on a pony."

"It is!" His words came out on a laugh. "Ross was right. Riding one is a lot easier than a horse."

Another small miracle.

After flashing Ross a grateful glance, she lifted her gaze to the rugged, fit cowboy trailing behind them. He looked as if he'd been born in the saddle. Even from the distance separating them, his eyes burned a brilliant blue. He tipped his black hat with a smile. "Mrs. Wentworth!"

She smiled. "It's Kit. I'm so happy to meet you at last, Mr. Lundgren."

"Call me Carson. Your son's a fine horseman," he said on a cough.

Kit liked the owner already. "That's so nice to hear. As his mother, I'm afraid I'm biased."

He grinned. "Of course. For our first time I thought we'd ride to the south pasture. It's not far and the kids will enjoy seeing part of the herd."

"Sounds terrific."

With Carson in the lead, they left the corral taking a different trail from the riders she'd seen earlier. He kept up a running conversation with the kids. Ross dropped back to her side. They followed the others, meandering in and out of the forested area of the ranch. The underbrush was full of small animal life, delighting her. Ross looked over at her. "You've got a mysterious smile on your face. What's that all about?"

"You'll think I'm silly if I tell you."

"Try me."

Ross was so easy to talk to. "When I was a young teen, I think I read every Louis L'Amour book ever published. As you know, that included his novels about Hopalong. Riding through this forest is like reliving some of them. I've got gooseflesh. Look!"

His eyes roved over her arms, taking all of her in at the same time without being obvious about it. "Carson's going to have fun talking to you. He has a library full of them at his house."

"You're kidding!"

"Nope. I still have a backache from carrying the collection into his new house." She chuckled. "It'll be interesting to hear the two of you compare notes on your favorite books."

"Because we were coming to a ranch, I brought several Louis L'Amours and a Jack London to read to Andy if he'll let me."

"*Call of the Wild* is one I'd love to be reading for the first time."

"I feel the same way. Jack London is another American author I particularly like. Andy has always wanted a dog, but his grandparents haven't allowed one. I think he'll like that book. The trouble is, he struggles a little in reading. Now that we're here, I hope to help him get more interested in books. My grandmother read to me and it got me turned on to it."

"How old were you when your parents were killed?"

"Eight."

"That's a tough age to lose your parents."

"Just a year younger than Andy."

"He's lucky to have you."

She was starting to feel emotional again and turned her head away. How was she ever going to repay these men for what they were doing for her and Andy?

Before long they came to an open meadow dotted with cattle. The sight of the herd combined with lowing sounds communicated a feeling of peace she relished.

Ross sidled next to her. "Another part of the herd is up on the mountain. We'll ride up there another day."

While she took it all in, her son rode over to her. The kids followed him. "See that border collie with the stockman, Mom?"

"Yes. He really keeps that herd in line."

"That's Buster," Johnny explained.

"I wish I had a dog."

"I know you do, honey." He would never know the losing arguments she'd had with the in-laws about letting Andy have a pet. Florence had no need for animals that she didn't deem "useful".

At that point the children got into a discussion about dogs while they watched Buster do his job. Carson gave out snacks and bottled water from his saddlebag. After another half hour had passed, he suggested they head back to the ranch.

While Ross rode next to Kit, Carson closed in on her other side, and the kids rode in front of them. "You're a good rider, too."

"Thanks. It's the horse beneath me. But it's also this ranch and everything that goes with it. You live in cowboy heaven." The men laughed. "I think I died and went there. With the Tetons looming over us, this is Bendigo Shafter country."

Carson's eyes lit up. "Aha! I can see you and I have a lot to talk about."

"Told you." Ross's aside made her smile.

Johnny turned in the saddle looking confused. "Who's that Bingo guy?" That kid had ears in the back of his head.

The men roared with laughter. Kit tried to suppress hers. Johnny was so cute. "He's a person in a book I love."

"Is he a cowboy like my dad?"

"Come to think of it, he *is*." Bigger than life, like these men.

"My mom loves to read," Andy piped up. His comment shocked Kit because he had been so withdrawn and rarely interjected into conversation.

"So do I!" Jenny exclaimed.

"What's one of your favorite books, honey?"

"The Goose Girl."

"Goose Girl!" Johnny started laughing.

"I've read it. That author won an award," Kit said.

"It's really good. Nana helps me with the hard words."

"Andy and I will have to read it."

"You can borrow it. I have it in my room."

"Thank you. And maybe one evening you guys would like me to read a chapter of *Call of the Wild* to you. It's great, too."

"What's it about?" Jenny wanted to know.

"A very special dog."

"Is he a terrier like mine?"

She shook her head at Johnny. "No. He's a cross between a collie and a Saint Bernard with the name Buck, the same as your daddy, Jenny. He gets stolen and sold to a trainer of sled dogs in Alaska. The man is kind, but then he dies. I won't tell you the rest."

"Let's do it tonight in the games room while we eat popcorn and drink sodas." Ross's suggestion excited the children.

Andy's gaze sought hers. "Can we, Mom?"

What? Was this her glum son from a day ago? "We're here to have fun. Right?"

He nodded.

Johnny and Jenny shouted hooray.

Carson made an unexpected announcement. "After

we get back we'll go for a swim and have a water fight before dinner."

"You're on," Kit heard Ross say.

No doubt they did this sort of thing all the time. They lived on an exciting plane she'd forgotten existed.

The six of them headed for the barn in the distance. Johnny rode next to Andy. "Tonight's the barbecue. Do you like ribs?"

"What are those?"

"Beef you eat off the bone," Kit explained. "I'm afraid Andy's grandparents don't eat barbecued ribs."

"Oh. They're really nummy."

"And messy," Jenny piped up. Both she and Johnny giggled.

Kit smiled at them. "Even so, my mouth is watering for some already. You're going to love them, Andy."

By the time they returned the horses to the barn, it was decided they'd all get their swimming gear and meet at the pool. Carson and Johnny left the barn in the Jeep.

Ross dropped off Jenny at the ranch house before driving Kit and Andy back to the cabin.

"I'll be by for you in half an hour, unless you need more time."

"We don't need more time, do we, Mom?"

Again her son's question took her by surprise. He actually sounded eager. Johnny and Jenny were a lot of fun. Not for the first time did she wish she'd had another baby so Andy wouldn't be an only child. It was a different world growing up without siblings. Kit ought to know. She would have loved a brother or sister to confide in.

"No. We'll be ready. In fact there's no need for you to come and get us. We'll meet you at the pool."

He tipped his hat. "See you soon, then."

After he drove off they went inside. She spotted her phone lying on the table. With a sense of dread she reached for it and discovered four messages, three from her in-laws and one from Nila Thornton in Texas. Kit checked her watch. It was ten after four.

She would call her friend tonight but decided she'd better phone her in-laws now. There wouldn't be time later. First she freshened up and put on her bikini beneath a change of jeans and a crew neck sweater. While Andy was changing, she phoned them without listening to the messages.

"Hello, Charles? How are you?"

"Never mind me. Why haven't you answered any of our calls?"

"We've been out riding most of the day. Now we're going to take a swim before dinner."

"I want to speak to Andy."

"Just a minute." Her son had just walked in the living room. She handed him the phone.

"Hello?"

It took a long time before Andy could get a word in. "But we just barely got here, Grandfather."

His comment gave Kit a jolt.

This was the first time she'd ever heard her son argue with Charles. She was incredulous. A subtle change had come over Andy. For him not to fall in line with his grandfather's wishes meant he was really enjoying this vacation.

"But Ross has all this fun stuff planned." *Ross.* After

another minute Andy handed her the phone. "He wants to talk to you," he whispered. "I don't want to go home yet."

Kit's adrenaline kicked in. "We're not leaving," she whispered back before saying hello to Charles once more. "I'm sorry, but we have to hang up now so we won't be late for dinner. We'll call you tomorrow. Good night."

Once she'd hung up, Andy stared at her in apprehension. "He's mad at me."

"No, honey, I'm the one he's upset with." Thank heaven. She put an arm around his shoulders. "Let's not let it spoil our trip. You know what he's like, but he'll get over it." *If only that were true.* "Shall we go?" Remembering the plans for after dinner, she wrapped up the Jack London book in some towels and they left.

Ross ran into Buck's wife, Alex, in the downstairs hallway. She smiled when she saw him. "Thanks for looking after Jenny. She had a wonderful time today. Apparently our newest young guest is a good rider."

"He's a good swimmer, too."

"So I hear." She handed him a folded note. "I took a message for you at the front desk. See you at the pool in a few minutes." Alex covered the counter when they needed help.

"Thanks." He took the stairs two at a time to his room. After a quick shower he'd change into his swimsuit. But first he looked at the message. The name Charles Wentworth caused him to pause in his tracks.

Why would he be calling the ranch? Surely he had

his daughter-in-law's cell phone number. He pressed the digits and waited.

"This is Charles Wentworth."

Ross blinked. The man sounded like Ross's father who, without preamble, assumed everyone knew who he was and expected to be catered to.

"Ross Livingston here." He could be just as peremptory. He'd learned from a master who'd happened to be his own father. "I understand you wished to talk to one of us in charge at the dude ranch. How can I help you?"

"You're the one I want to speak to about Andrew."

"He's a fine boy."

"Andrew's the reason I'm calling. Can you guarantee his safety for the rest of the time he's with you?"

Ross frowned. Could anyone? It was an odd question. What about *Kit's* safety? "We're doing our best. Being retired marines, we've never had a problem protecting our guests."

"I'm afraid that's not going to be good enough in an environment like yours. After our trip to Norway, I shouldn't have allowed Kathryn to take him."

Allowed? He held the phone tighter. "Why not?"

"Let's just say she shouldn't be there on her own and needs watching. I told her I want my grandson home by midweek and I expect you to make it happen. Do I make myself clear? Otherwise I'll hold you personally responsible."

For what?

Ross could feel hackles rising on the back of his neck. Nothing caused his blood to boil faster than a bullying tactic. Ross's father had tried that once too often until he'd gone into the military out of his parent's reach. As far as he was concerned, Charles Wentworth was of the same ilk as his father and could go to hell.

"Surely that will be up to your daughter-in-law to decide."

"Do you know who you're talking to?"

Ross had had enough. "You'll have to take this up with her. Now I'm afraid duty calls. Goodbye."

He was full of adrenaline after getting off the phone. *She needs watching.* What in the hell did that mean? Was there something wrong with her? With Andy? The man had sounded positively feudal. As he thought about their conversation, Ross grimaced, not liking some of the thoughts he was having.

By the time he got ready and went down to the pool, his good mood had been altered. He was riddled with questions that needed answering, but that couldn't happen until tonight after Andy went to bed.

The patio was filled with guests taking advantage of the late afternoon sun. The weather was perfect for the barbecue they held every weekend for all their dude ranch guests. He didn't see Andy or Kit. Maybe they hadn't arrived yet or were still in the cabana.

A few guests were swimming in the pool. His gaze traveled the length of it until he spotted a dark-haired woman with a heavenly body treading water in the deep end. The top half of the light blue bikini she filled out was barely visible. *Kit.*

Two males, probably in their twenties, had closed in to talk to her. Whether they were there on their own or with girlfriends, Ross had no idea. All he could see was that they were enjoying themselves and eating her alive with their eyes.

No sin had been committed, but an unfamiliar sensation attacked Ross in the gut. Driven by another gush of pure adrenaline, he dropped his towel on a chair and dived deep to reach those beautiful legs keeping her afloat.

"Ross!" She half laughed in surprise when he rose out of the water next to her. In that first instant, he saw pleasure flash in those deep green orbs. Enough to satisfy him she wasn't indifferent to him.

"How are you this evening, Mrs. Wentworth?" He'd stressed the "Mrs." so the two guys surrounding her would get the point. That brought another laugh from her.

"I'm fine, Mr. Livingston." She gave as good as she got. He liked that.

"Where's Andy?"

"He went with Buck to find Jenny."

Good ol' Buck. "So, who are your friends?" he asked without taking his eyes off her. Wet and *sans* makeup, she was a lovely sight.

"I don't know who you mean." But a slow smile spread over the classic features of her face. "I guess you frightened off some of your guests when you surfaced like a submarine in enemy waters."

"They shouldn't have let their guard down." His pulse had taken off with dizzying speed. "Did I ruin anything important?"

"Well…if they had any plans, you successfully sabotaged them. Something you learned in the marines?"

It was his turn to laugh, which provoked a cough.

Her smile was replaced by a look of anxiety. "Does the water make your condition worse?"

"That depends on who's in it with me."

She was quiet for a minute before she said, "Aren't you ever serious?"

Where she was concerned, he was becoming serious way too fast. Now this phone call from her father-in-law was raising questions that wouldn't leave him alone.

"How about a race to the other end of the pool?"

Fire lit her eyes. "You're on!"

The battle had begun. They had to swim out and around a couple of guests to reach the shallow end. She was an excellent swimmer, a skill no doubt developed by spending many hours at the Wentworth mansion swimming pool. He had to pour it on to save face and came up coughing.

"Way to go, Mom! You beat Ross!" Andy had reappeared with Jenny.

"That's because he let me." Out of breath, she hugged the edge of the pool. Kit's gaze switched to her son. "You know what? The sun has gone down, and they're setting up for the barbecue. Let's change back into our clothes."

"Can't Andy swim with us a little longer?" Jenny stared at her expectantly.

"Sure. Do you want to, honey?"

He nodded. "Let's do dives off the board."

Johnny jumped up and down. "We'll play follow the leader."

The children took off for the deep end, leaving Ross alone with Kit. Everyone else was getting out of the pool. "You're a great swimmer."

A tantalizing half smile broke the corner of her mouth. "You want to know what's really great? The way you handled Andy today *without* handling him, if you know what I mean."

He cocked his head. "I'm afraid he's like me. I don't respond well to authority." The phone call with Charles Wentworth was a case in point.

"That's because you're your own person with the strength of your convictions. I'd like to see my son grow up like that. Now if you'll excuse me, I'm going to get changed."

THE AIR HAD grown a little cooler, but that wasn't the reason Kit had the shivers as she showered and washed her hair. What she'd just said to Ross had sounded too personal, but she couldn't seem to control her thoughts or feelings. There'd been times in the pool when the way Ross had looked at her had sent a weakness through her limbs.

During their swim their bodies had brushed against each other. Every time there'd been contact, it had felt as if she'd been branded with liquid fire. If she wasn't mistaken, she noticed Andy starting to form an attachment to him. But Kit had a different problem because attached wasn't a strong enough word for what was happening inside of her whenever he came near.

She wanted him to kiss her, hold her.

You want him, Kit.

It was true, and there was no point in denying it. But she was mortified. These retired marines had honored Winn's memory by inviting her and Andy to the ranch for a week of fun-filled activities. Yet here she was, behaving as anything but her husband's grieving widow.

When she'd first met Winn, there'd been a strong

physical attraction, but within a few years of their marriage it had died. To experience desire this powerful after years of feeling dead inside was so painful in its intensity, she was alarmed by it.

Over the years of charity work she'd done, there'd been a lot of attractive men she'd worked with. She could say the same for many of the waiters and staff at the various country clubs the family frequented. Several of the golf pros who'd given her lessons were exceptionally charming. The captain and crew of Charles's favorite yacht were big flirts and a subject of conversation with the women of her in-laws' social circle invited on board.

Most of the men coming and going or passing through Kit's life under those circumstances were open to a flirtation and gave off signals. If she'd ever been inclined and hadn't clung to a strong set of morals, she could have had affairs with any number of them. That included some of Charles's own male friends who stayed over on weekends and had grown bored with their own wives.

Yet it was the tall, striking Wyoming cowboy communicating his seeming disdain of her the minute she'd met him in the terminal yesterday who'd set off hormones she didn't know she had. For an aloof stranger to have that kind of power over her—to care what he thought—meant something monumental had happened to her.

She had to do something to fight these feelings for him, starting right now! He was the kind of real man a woman dreamed about—a man so far out of her reach it was ludicrous.

"Mom?"

She wheeled around with her hair brush in hand. "Hey—had enough swimming?"

"Yeah. Ross sent me in here to get dressed. He wants us to hurry before all the food is gone."

"They won't run out of food. He was just teasing."

"I know."

Her pulse raced at the thought of being with Ross. Unfortunately she couldn't stop her nervous system from reacting over anything to do with him. In two days of being on the Teton Valley Ranch with him, she'd run a gamut of emotions that now included her own brand of hero worship coupled with an ache for him that was building inside her.

"Why don't you take a quick shower while I finish doing my hair?"

"Okay."

In a minute they were ready. She left the cabana with her book under her arm. Lots of suntanned, happy guests seated around enjoying the candlelit barbecue nodded at them as they made their way to the banquet table.

Kit noticed Ross over at one of the larger tables with his partners and their families. Her heart skipped a beat as he waved to her. She smiled back before remembering she wasn't going to pay him any undue attention.

The smorgasbord featured everything from barbecued ribs to steaks and all the trimmings. Kit found she was hungry. "Let's take a little of everything, Andy. What you don't want, I'll eat."

With their plates full, they walked over to Ross's table. He introduced Kit to Alex, Buck's wife, a lovely chestnut-blonde woman, then he helped her and Andy to be seated. When she felt his hand graze her shoulders, it almost melted her on the spot.

The fun dinner conversation helped her to relax. Out of the corner of her eye she noticed that her son seemed to be enjoying himself. During the delicious dessert of fresh huckleberry pie, Tracy brought up the plans for the next day.

"Alex and I thought it would be fun to take the children into Jackson for lunch and a movie. After tomorrow there won't be any more matinees. We thought we'd make an afternoon of it to celebrate the end of summer before they have to go back to school. If you and Andy would like to come, you'd be welcome."

She waited for her son to whisper he didn't want to go, but he didn't say anything.

"Thank you, Tracy. Will it be all right if we tell you in the morning?"

"Of course. We'll be leaving around eleven-thirty in the van."

"Sounds fun," Carson said, kissing Tracy's cheek. Kit could tell they had that rare kind of love. Her glance fell on Buck who'd brought his wife another helping of food. The tender way they looked at each other was truly something to witness. As for Ross and everything he was doing for Kit and Andy, there were no words.

She thought back to her marriage with Winn. It had failed before it ever got off the ground, but she shouldn't be comparing him to these men. Her husband had been raised under such difficult emotional circumstances it was amazing he'd survived to adulthood.

Now had come the time for her and Andy to make

their own escape to survive. That's what she wanted for her son whom she hadn't seen this animated since he was a much younger boy. Her gaze lit on Ross who was making it all possible. Right now he was using his phone so Andy could look at the list of movies playing in Jackson.

There was no finer man anywhere. It would take an exceptional woman to win his heart. Whoever she was, she'd be the luckiest person on earth. Kit knew deep down in her soul she could never be that woman. She was Winn's widow, and she already had a growing child.

Apparently the rare woman he needed to meet hadn't come along yet. He deserved one who'd never been married. Ross could start his own family with her. Someone who didn't have all Kit's baggage. Being Charles Wentworth's daughter-in-law presented problems no man would want to deal with. She lowered her eyes and drank the rest of her coffee.

Carson was the first one to get up. "It's time for a bedtime story from Kit. Let's go to the games room."

Kit watched Andy walk with the kids instead of holding back and telling her he didn't want to do anything. The change in him was too remarkable to be an aberration. She knew the reason why....

While the others took their places on the two leather couches, Andy sat on the love seat next to Ross. That left Kit, who sat in the big leather chair. She opened the book and laid the groundwork for the story about the dog named Buck. Kit had been afraid she'd lose the kids' attention, but they sat there intrigued by the animal's thoughts of his wonderful life with Judge Miller.

Halfway through the first chapter she shut the book, knowing it was better to quit while the children were still enjoying the story. They protested of course.

Jenny was totally caught up in it. "Something bad is going to happen to him, huh, Kit?"

"We'll have to keep reading to find out."

"Will you read to us tomorrow night?" Johnny asked.

"I'd love to. I'd rather read than just about anything."

Everyone got up. Carson thanked her. "That'll give us something to look forward to tomorrow night. Say good-night, kids."

Ross nodded to her. "If you're ready, let's go."

She turned to Andy. "Would you run to the cabana and get our suits and towels, please? We'll meet you at the truck."

"Sure." He took off.

As Ross walked her outside and helped her into the cab, his hand gripped her upper arm. "Kit? We need to talk." All of a sudden his voice sounded an octave lower than usual.

She turned her head to look at him. Obviously something was wrong. How could anything be wrong on this beautiful night? "What is it?"

Long black lashes half shuttered the enigmatic look coming from his dark eyes. "After the phone call I received earlier from the timber king Charles Cavanaugh Wentworth, maybe it's just as well his grandson isn't around to hear this."

Oh, no.

The long reaching arm of her father-in-law didn't miss anything or anyone.

Chapter Five

Ross's news caused her to lose color. That as much as anything verified his suspicion that something ugly was going on.

Beneath her fetching brunette hair, still damp from a shampooing, he found himself staring into a pair of the same sea-green eyes that had beguiled him from the beginning, but right now they looked haunted.

"You know about him."

"I know his ancestor amassed a fortune in timber in the mid-1800s and his legacy grew from there."

"What did he say to you?" she asked quietly.

Though he'd managed to frighten the hell out of her, he had to admire her for maintaining her dignity. *Nothing but the truth, Livingston.* This was no time for games. "He wanted to make sure nothing happens to his grandson and ordered me to make sure you fly home midweek, or else...."

"Oh, no—" He felt the shudder that passed through her body. "W-What did you tell him?" she stammered.

"I told him we know how to keep our guests safe. Before I rang off, I explained that the decision for you to leave was up to you."

Her dark head reared back. *"You hung up on him?"*

The fear in her voice hit him in the gut. "In a manner of speaking."

A small cry escaped her lips before she turned away. Slipping into marine mode, Ross grasped her other arm, forcing her to look at him.

She presented a pinched white face to him. "Please, let me go before someone sees us."

"Not yet," he ground out. "I understand you're in some kind of trouble."

Panic filled her eyes. "I wish to heaven he hadn't called the ranch, but now that he has, this mustn't become your problem. I couldn't bear it."

"I'm afraid it already is." After witnessing her shock, he saw all the signs of someone planning to cut and run. He'd done it himself years ago and could relate.

"Please, don't say that." Her voice shook.

"I *have* to. After Andy's in bed asleep and we're alone, you're going to tell me what's going on. For the moment you need to present a calm front so he doesn't get alarmed. When we get back to the cabin, ask me to come in and watch TV with you. Hopefully he'll get tired and go to bed."

Another shudder wracked her lovely body before the fight went out of her, and she nodded. Reasonably confident she could see the wisdom in his plan, he let go of her arm and walked around to get in the truck. Andy was back in a flash and they were off.

When they drew up to the cabin, it was her son who asked him if he'd come in and watch the movie *Shrek* with them.

"I haven't seen that one."

"There's a donkey in it that's pretty funny."

"A donkey? That I have to see."

Andy preceded them into the cabin carrying the plastic bag with their swimsuits.

"Why don't you get ready for bed first, honey?"

"Okay."

For the next hour and a half Ross watched the entertaining film and laughed in the same parts with Andy. Kit pretended to be involved, but Ross knew she wasn't seeing anything. When it was over, she got up and turned it off.

"Time for bed, honey."

"I know."

Ross stood. "See you in the morning at breakfast, Andy. If you want to go fishing, Buck will take you."

He nodded. "Thanks."

"Good night."

Kit gave her son a hug. After he disappeared into the other part of the cabin and shut the door, she walked back and sat down on the couch with a wooden expression.

With his voice lowered, he said, "Before I ask you anything else, I need to know something. Has your father-in-law ever laid a hand on you or Andy?"

She smoothed the hair out of her eyes. "No," she answered in a quiet tone. "He's not like that and doesn't need to use physical force. He can merely guilt you into doing what he wants."

Those were the same tactics Ross's father had used on him. Though it shouldn't mean anything of a personal nature to him, he felt a sense of relief hearing it. "I may not know all the facts, but it's clear you're in a tense situation."

She got up from the couch again, hugging her arms to her waist. "We are, and I'm sorry you're involved in any way after inviting us here out of the kindness of your hearts. It isn't fair to you."

"Why don't you let me be the judge of that."

"When your letter came, I was deeply touched to think you soldiers would do such a wonderful thing for Andy. It meant so much to me, even if he doesn't truly understand the great honor you've shown us. I wanted to come more than you know and prayed my father-in-law wouldn't try to stand in the way."

Ross shook his head. "He's *that* controlling?"

"He's always been controlling, but since Winn's death he's been much worse. They have two married daughters, but Winn was their only son. They've been so grief-stricken, they've started to think of Andy as their own son.

"When I received your letter, I told him we were going to accept. He told me I couldn't because they had that cruise in Norway planned. It was just an excuse, of course. He didn't want us going anywhere. That's why I called the ranch and asked if Andy and I could come for the first week of September. Mr. Lundgren was wonderful about it.

"While we were in Norway, my in-laws tried to get me to cancel my plans. They worked on Andy, knowing he didn't want to come to Wyoming. It's my opinion that for him to think of being around some retired marines who'd survived the war was simply too painful for him. At that juncture I took matters into my own hands.

"After we returned to the hotel in Oslo, I left a note

for them at the front desk telling them Andy and I had flown back to the States and would be in Wyoming for the next week. Because it was an earlier flight, that's why we arrived in Jackson at three instead of six-thirty.

"Andy was unhappy about it, but I gave him no choice. Since our arrival, all that has changed and he's becoming a different child."

Ross rubbed his lower lip with his thumb. "I'm glad to hear it. Go on."

"What do you mean?"

"What else aren't you telling me?" he questioned. "You've already let me know that Mr. Wentworth isn't physically violent with you, so what's really happening here?"

"I'd rather not get into it. I'm ashamed enough as it is. Already I'm sure you're sorry that you ever invited us."

Ross grimaced. "Forget about that. Since genes don't lie, you two are definitely mother and son. Now I need the answer to another question." He hated asking it, but he had to know before he made another move.

"Do your in-laws have custody of Andy? Remember that lying to me at this stage won't do you any good. Is that why he was warning me about you?"

"Warning? In what way?"

"He said you needed watching and he shouldn't have let you come."

She drew in her breath, as if she was holding herself in check. "Charles will stoop to any level to achieve want he wants."

"What *does* he want?" Ross prodded her.

"He wants Andy to be the son he lost!"

"There's more to it than that for him to phone the ranch asking for one of us in charge."

A tortured moan escaped her. "No—I mean there *is* a reason, but it's not what you think."

"Then explain it to me."

"I—I don't know where to start," she stammered. "It's complicated."

"Nightmares usually are. I've got all night, and you're my responsibility while you're here."

"I don't want you mixed up in this."

His temper flared. "I already am. Does he have a case against you for being an unfit mother?"

He heard her sharp intake of breath. "In his mind he does."

Ross felt like he'd been kicked in the gut. "On what grounds?"

"Grounds?" she cried out. "Winn married me without his parents' approval. I was beneath their social class and not the woman they'd picked out for him. Because of guilt, he insisted we live with them at the mansion to make up for it.

"They wanted the marriage annulled, but by then I was pregnant. I thought our living situation was temporary, but it turned out to be permanent. I was a nineteen-year-old without an education from Wellesley or Vassar. I didn't have the right stuff. I didn't come from a family with money or connections."

Ross was listening. In the lofty circles of the Wentworths and the Livingstons, the right background was of vital importance. He closed his eyes tightly for a moment. He got it. Because of his own highly privileged background, Ross got it with a vengeance.

"*That* made me an unfit mother for a Wentworth, but they adored Andy and took over the parenting, especially when Winn was away. Since his death, everything has been so much worse. I told them I planned to get Andy and me a place of our own because we need to be independent.

"The thought of it has upset them so much, they've refused to discuss it. He has warned me that if I leave the mansion, he'll cut me off without a penny. That wouldn't bother me, but I have to think of Andy's future. I argued with Charles and Florence about it before the trip to Norway. He called tonight because he's afraid I might actually move out."

"And are you?"

"Yes. I have it all planned. But I haven't told Andy."

Ross shook his head. "You mean he knows nothing?"

"Not yet. Since Carson's letter inviting us here, I've been making preparations. But nothing can happen until I have a talk with my son. I believe I know how he feels deep inside, but I've got to find the right time to get the truth out of him."

"If he's amenable, what's your plan?"

"When we leave the ranch, we'll fly to Galveston, Texas."

Galveston? Ross's mind reeled. That's where he had his own beach pad, but he hadn't used it in years. He paid a company to keep it cleaned and allowed needy college students to live there. It was an hour and a half away from his family's home in Houston.

"Why Galveston?"

"My hairdresser's daughter Nila lives there and has

her own shop. When she visits her mother, who married an easterner, she comes to work with her and gives me a special manicure and pedicure. Over the years we've become good friends. She has a daughter Andy's age and they're friends, too.

"She's put me in touch with the owner of a small bookstore who's retiring and isn't going through a Realtor. I've always wanted to own one. Books are my fetish. I'm hoping to find an investor to go into business with me. I have some savings to keep Andy and me going for a while."

A while? Good grief!

"I've done my research and have written up a business plan that includes running a coffee bar with it."

"That's very enterprising of you. A coffee bar is an excellent idea." But she would need an investor with a hefty sum, or she'd never get the loan in the first place. A lot of small bookstores were going out of business.

"There's a suitable apartment complex nearby that Nila has checked out for me. I'm planning to fly there and look everything over. There's only one problem. It *is* just an idea, and if it doesn't work out, we'll do something else. But the truth is, Andy and I can't live with his grandparents any longer. They're swallowing us alive. I don't intend to cut them out of our lives. I'd never do that, but we need our own space now."

"And Andy feels the same?"

"Maybe I'm wrong, but I believe he wants his freedom as much as I do. Though I can't imagine it, if Andy can't bring himself to leave his grandparents, even if it means he has to go away to that school, then we'll fly back to Maine when our trip is over."

Ross was so amazed by what he was hearing, he could hardly think. "Of course. It's not my place to offer an opinion."

"You have every right after the way my father-in-law spoke to you."

Kɪᴛ ᴡᴀs ᴇᴍʙᴀʀʀᴀssᴇᴅ because she was about to lose it in front of this incredible man. "Since Winn's death ten months ago, they've exerted total power over my son. With systematic precision, they've been taking him away from me piece by piece."

"How could they do that?"

"Because my husband and I married in a private ceremony in Rhode Island without his family while he was on leave from the military. He'd said it was the way he wanted it. My grandmother had died with only $3,000 in the bank. I was alone, too naive for words. Once we'd gone on a short honeymoon, he took me to his parents' mansion to meet them.

"They would have gotten a judge to annul our marriage, but by then I was pregnant. Since I was carrying a Wentworth, that changed everything. Tragically, our marriage disintegrated. We ended up living with them against my wishes. I've never been able to leave since."

Ross studied her with enigmatic dark eyes, not saying anything.

"They've run my life and Andy's day after day for years, turning him into a Wentworth robot. With Winn gone so much on deployments, the grandparents took over raising him as if I scarcely existed. I wanted to leave years ago, but I was married with no means of support. Winn forbade me to get a job. Andy has no idea my love for his father died early in our marriage."

Good grief. "I'm sorry to hear that."

"It was a very unhappy time. They never forgave Winn for marrying me. That's why he insisted we live with them as his way of making it up to them. As for me, *I'm* the one they despised for luring their son into a marriage they found intolerable.

"The more Winn bent over backwards to make amends and placate his parents, the more the gulf between the two of us widened. I'm sure he had other women, but I can't prove it. And though I grieve over his death and grieve for Andy's sake, that world nearly destroyed me. It'll destroy Andy if I don't get us away from them."

He rubbed the back of his neck in a seemingly unconscious gesture. "What about Winn's siblings? Is Andy close to them?"

"Not really. Andy's male cousins are older and have little to do with him. Unfortunately, Charles and Florence dote on him to the point that I feel there's something intrinsically wrong with them. They're sick to cling to Andy as they do.

"I love my son so much, I can't say our marriage was a mistake, but divorce was out of the question because Winn would have gone to court to win custody of Andy if I'd left him, and he would have won. I couldn't let that happen."

"Do you have no one you can turn to closer to home?"

"Except for Nila and her husband, there's no one else I trust. You heard about that school they're sending him to. I told Winn how I felt about him being sent away from home, but he couldn't stand up to Charles about that or moving us out of the mansion. Only one man in a million could do it. Winn didn't have what it took.

"But what no one counted on was his getting killed in Afghanistan. His parents expect me to go on being his faithful, grieving widow who devotes her life to charitable causes. But it's no life, not for me or Andy." There was a finality in her tone. Ross believed her.

He shifted his weight. "My reply to your father-in-law didn't reassure him. What's to stop him from flying here to check up on you?"

"Absolutely nothing." She ground her teeth together. "So that means I'm going to have that talk with Andy when he wakes up in the morning. He's the key to everything. If he wants to continue living with his grandparents, then I'll phone them and tell them we'll be flying back to Maine after our trip.

"But if my son wants a new life with me, then we'll fly to Texas at the end of the week. After we get there, I'll let my in-laws know where we are. In either case, this cabin will be available for more of your regular guests and you won't have to be involved." Her voice held a tremor.

Ross sucked in his breath. "But I *am* involved!"

"I'm so sorry he threatened you. It isn't fair, not when you've done everything for us. Be assured I'll take care of the situation from here on out." She walked to the door and opened it.

His legs felt like lead as he moved toward her. "Are you going to be all right tonight?"

"Of course. I'm glad you told me about the phone

call. Talking to you has helped more than you know. Thank you for putting up with me and Andy. You've been a saint. God bless you and your partners for your goodness. Good night, Ross."

"Good luck with Andy."

Once back in the truck, he took off for the ranch house. After hearing about her plans, he felt so chewed up inside, he didn't know where to go with all his emotions.

Carson was just pulling away from the parking area in the Jeep, but when he saw Ross he braked and waited for him to catch up. "Hey, buddy—you look like a bull stomped on you."

"You could say that. I went a few rounds on the phone with Charles Wentworth earlier this evening."

Carson squinted at him. "What's going on?"

"You don't want to know."

"The hell I don't."

"Let's just say Kit's a widow with a big problem. I'll know a lot more tomorrow, then I'll fill you in." He coughed. "I'm not fit company right now. Go home to your family."

"You're sure? If you need to talk, Tracy would understand."

"I know she would. You're a lucky man. See you in the morning."

AFTER HER PHONE call to Nila, who was behind Kit a hundred percent and waiting for her and Andy to come to Texas, she went to bed. But she slept poorly, and her eyes popped open at six-thirty, anxious for Andy to wake up.

She lay on her side in the twin bed and watched him while he slept. He moved around a lot. One of his pillows had fallen on the floor, and part of his leg poked out from beneath the quilt.

His cowboy boots and socks lay on the carpet at the side of his bed where he'd taken everything off before collapsing under the covers. Yesterday had been a big day. Her dear, dear son. This morning would be their moment of truth.

She'd been rehearsing what she would say to him, but her stomach was in knots and nothing sounded right. Kit was about to ask him if he would like to leave the only home he'd ever known and trust her to make a new one for them. It terrified her to think what his answer might be.

Was it asking too much? Had she waited too long? Could he handle moving away from his grandparents and the home where his father had lived? Last night Ross had wished her good luck before he'd driven away. His comment had caused her a lot of tossing and turning because he knew she would need it.

Nila had encouraged her to open up her heart to Andy and hold nothing back, then wait for him to respond. Kit's grandmother would have given her the same counsel.

She heard his sheets rustle. Then, finally, she heard, "Mom?"

This was it. "Good morning, honey."

He raised himself up on one elbow. "How come you're still in bed?"

She'd always been an early riser, so she could understand his surprise. "I was waiting for you to wake up so we could talk."

Andy sat all the way up, leaning back against the headboard. "What about?" As usual, he sounded worried.

Kit's heart beat so fast it clogged up her throat. "About us."

"What do you mean?"

It was difficult to swallow. "Every day of your life I've told you how much I love you, that you're the most precious thing to me in my life. Now I'm going to ask you a question, and it's vitally important you tell me the truth. Do you love me? I mean *really* love me?" She couldn't remember the last time she'd heard him say it to her.

There was a long drawn-out silence. She had to wait ages before he said yes, without looking at her. He'd been closed up for so long, she feared he'd lost the capacity to share. Thank heaven for that admission, even if he couldn't say the words.

"I'm so happy you said that. Now I need you to be honest with me about another question I have. You know how I feel about you going away to boarding school. It will mean you and I won't get to see each other more than twice a month, if that. But the point is, how do *you* really feel about it?"

His gaze shot to hers. Those gray eyes went dark with emotion.

"Forget that your father wanted you to go there, honey. Forget that your grandmother and grandfather are insisting you go. Forget that your cousins Thomas and Jeremy went there. I want to know what *you* want. Whatever you tell me, I promise it will be our secret."

At first she wondered if he'd even heard her because he sat there so still. Then slowly he got out of bed in his camouflage pajamas and crept over to the window. She watched him looking at the Grand Teton for a long time before his shoulders started to shake.

"I…don't want to leave you, but Grandfather says I *have* to."

Thank heaven!

"No, you don't!"

Andy spun around with a shocked look on his tear-stained face. "I don't?"

"Come here, darling."

He ran over to her. She pulled him into her arms, and they lay on the bed, hugging so hard it almost knocked the breath out of her. Kit rocked him for a long time while he sobbed. Her heart broke to think he'd been carrying around this pain for so long.

"H-how can you stop him from making me go?" His voice faltered.

Her son understood too much. His question answered a lot of hers and gave her the backbone she needed. "Because you're *my* son. Now that your dad is gone, I don't want to live with your grandparents any longer. I love them, but I want us to find a place of our own and make our own decisions from now on."

He sat up. "Where?"

Her heart thumped so hard, she was certain he could hear it. "A place where I believe we could be happy."

For a minute there'd been a light in those wet eyes, but it suddenly dimmed. "He won't let us go." Just then he sounded so adult. Five little words. They told her Andy understood the kind of power his controlling grandfather wielded, and that he hated it. That was all she needed to know.

"He *has* to, honey. You're not his son. Your father was wrong to make us live with your grandparents. It was never what I wanted. We should have had our own home, but he insisted."

"Why?"

Oh, Andy. What to tell you without ruining your image of him.

"I think because he was the only son, he felt he had to stay with them. It's a shame they didn't encourage him to get out on his own the way your aunts did with their husbands. Instead your grandparents clung to him. But now that he's gone, you and I need to have our own home and live the way we want to live. Don't you agree?"

"Yes," he said in a solemn tone. "I love them, but I don't want to live with them all the time."

That was all she needed to know. "Then we won't. I've been planning this for a long time."

"You have?"

She nodded. "After you were born, I told your father I wanted to move out of the mansion and get our own place, but he said he couldn't do that to your grandparents."

"He was afraid of Grandfather."

Kit moaned inwardly. "Yes, honey. Charles can be a scary person when he wants his own way. But *you're* not afraid of him. I heard you on the phone with him yesterday. You told him you didn't want to leave the ranch yet. It's not his decision to make for us.

"Your grandparents have been wonderful. They've done everything for us, but now it's time for me to take care of us. I've saved some money."

"Really?" He sounded so happy, she couldn't believe it.

"It's not a lot, but it's enough to give us a start while I find us a place to live and get a job."

"What kind?"

"You know how much I love books. I'm hoping to buy a small bookstore and run it. There's one for sale in Galveston, Texas, where Nila lives. She has become a very good friend to me and I know how much you like her and Kim. There's an apartment close by where we could live."

"You mean we'll move to Texas?" He didn't sound thrilled about that.

"When we leave the ranch, we'll fly down and take a look. I already have our airline tickets. If we don't like the situation, then we'll put our heads together and decide where we want to go and what we want to do. If we like it, then your grandparents can come and visit when they want. I want you to be happy with this decision, otherwise we won't do it."

"But we won't go back to Grandfather's—"

"No, darling. That's over."

"Promise?"

That said it all. "Promise. But there's just one problem."

"What?"

"Your grandfather phoned Ross yesterday."

"He did?"

"Yes. He said he didn't like us being gone for so long and told Ross to send us home right away."

Andy gave a carefree laugh. "Ross wouldn't do that. He's not afraid of anything."

Nope. Andy had already sized up their host and knew exactly how amazing he was. "No. He told Charles that the decision to stay or leave was entirely up to you and me."

"I bet Grandfather's mad at him."

"I'm sure he is. It means your grandfather might fly here on his private jet before our vacation is over."

"Ross will protect us. He's nice, Mom."

"I agree." Andy had never applied that adjective to anyone he knew, especially not his stuffed shirt uncles who were too caught up in their own self-importance by marrying into the Wentworth family to show much attention to Andy. They jumped when Charles said jump. Poor Andy. After living with his iron-willed grandfather, Andy could see Ross was like the difference between night and day. The three of them had been together 24/7 since they'd arrived here.

"He's so cool. I wish he weren't sick."

"It's not the kind of sick that has put him and his partners to bed. It's more of a condition, honey. But you have to admire them for not letting it get in the way of living their lives. Now, let's get dressed and hurry to the ranch house for breakfast. I'm starving."

"Me, too." He jumped off the bed. "I'm glad Ross will be here if Grandfather comes."

"Honey—" she said in exasperation, "Ross has nothing to do with this. I'll deal with your grandfather and tell him you and I have other plans. He can't make us do anything. I'll tell him that when we're settled, we'll let them know. Hopefully when he and Florence see that we mean it, they'll understand and we'll all get along better."

"Does Ross know we're going to Texas?"

Ross again. She remembered Andy's reaction to Carson's letter they'd received in July. *They're a bunch of lame marines. I hate them.* There'd been an enormous change in her son's attitude since then.

"Yes. Just remember this is our business. Please, don't talk about this to him or the other kids."

"I won't. But what if Grandfather finds out we went to Texas?"

"He won't know where to look for us."

"How come?" he asked.

"Close your eyes. When I'm ready, I'll tell you to open them. Go on and do it for me. It's a surprise. Please?"

"Okay."

When they were closed, she ran in the bedroom and pulled a wig and a hat out of her suitcase. After she returned, she put the wig on.

"You can open them now."

He did her bidding, then blinked several times in sheer disbelief. Finally came the outburst. *"Mom—"*

"How do you like me with blond hair?" While he stood there speechless, she plopped the green sojourner hat with the wide rim on his head. "That covers your hair. People may think you're a cancer patient. Run in the bathroom and take a look."

He acted stunned before darting off. Andy used to

like games when he was too young to understand what was going on. "Hey—it's cool!" he shouted from the other room. She hardly recognized such enthusiasm.

"I think so, too. When we leave here, we'll be different. See, honey? No one's going to be looking for a mother with blond hair and her son wearing that kind of hat. We'll wear these disguises until we get to our destination." He looked at her, and she looked at him before they burst into laughter and hugged like two crazy people.

On her way out of the room for a shower, her cell phone rang. Andy was closest to the bedside table and reached for it. "It's Grandfather."

"I'll get it." With everything out in the open, Kit was no longer afraid to talk in front of Andy. She walked back and took it from him. "Good morning, Charles."

"I'm glad you answered. I'm calling early because there's a flight leaving Jackson at eleven o'clock this morning for Denver. Your connecting flight will have you home by evening. I've already made the changes to your tickets."

Kit sank down on the side of her bed. "Is Florence on the line?"

"Why?"

"Because I want both of you to hear what I have to say at the same time."

"Just a minute."

She waited until her mother-in-law got on the phone. "What do you want to talk to us about?"

"I have something to tell you. If you decide to hang up on me before I'm finished, then I'm sorry for that. When Winn brought me into your home ten years ago,

I thought we would only be staying with you for a few weeks until we got our own home. But that never happened. Now that he's gone, I need to make a home for Andy and me."

Her son stood by her, watching and listening.

"You have a home!" Florence cried.

"Yes, but it's not mine, as I've reminded you many times. Andy and I love you. We're grateful for everything you've done for us, but it's time for me to build a new life with my son."

"I've heard enough from you!" Charles blurted before she heard a click. That was no surprise.

"Florence, are you still there?"

"Yes," came the brittle response.

"Andy and I are going to finish out this week of our vacation. When we leave the ranch, we won't be coming home."

A heart-wrenching cry escaped. This was as hard as anything she'd ever done.

"As soon as I've found us a place to live and get a job, I'll phone you and let you know. Once we're settled, I'll send for our things. There's no reason why we can't visit each other often for the rest of our lives. Andy loves you and the family, but we need our space. Can you understand that?"

"No, I can't. We've given you everything!"

"I know and I'm indebted to you, but now it's time for me to give my son everything the way you did for Winn."

"But you have no skills, no resources. Nothing. How can you possibly care for our grandson?"

Well it wasn't for want of trying. After all these years, that comment still hurt.

"I love my son and have the brains and the will to take care of him. The rest will come. I'm promising you now that we'll talk often and see each other whenever we can. Is there anything else you want to say to me before we hang up?"

Her question got lost because she heard Charles in the background. Florence was sobbing to him.

Kit clicked off and felt Andy's arms go around her. His love was all that was sustaining her right now.

Chapter Six

Ross had slept poorly and awakened at five, too restless to lie in bed. It was almost impossible to believe how much life had changed since Saturday. Thirty odd hours had passed, and already he was caught up in someone else's trial of fire.

After showering and dressing in a polo shirt and jeans, he'd gone down to the office to put out the payroll. A couple of faxes had arrived in response to his queries about the natural gas drilling project. He planned to meet one of the men from the oil company at the site on Carson's property later in the morning. While he was sending a fax back verifying their arrangement, the guys joined him.

He coughed as his partners filed in the room. They usually assembled in the ranch office early. This morning they sat on the chairs with their legs extended, hands behind their heads, staring at him expectantly. Carson said, "Let's talk about the widow with the big problem."

Ross found a spot on the end of the desk and gripped the edge with his hands. "Guys? When I joined up with you in this venture, you knew all about me and my background. Now let me tell you Kit's story." For the next ten minutes he held his audience captive, leaving nothing out. When he'd finished with another cough, he stood up.

"There are only two differences between her story and mine. My father isn't a sick tyrant, just misguided. She wasn't born a Wentworth, but she'll always be in hell because she gave birth to one, and her father-in-law doesn't know when to give up. I think he or one of his bodyguard types is going to fly into Jackson and make a scene here soon.

"I made the mistake of ticking him off when he phoned yesterday. Kit hasn't exaggerated a thing. He's dangerous because he's abusive and won't stop hammering her until he gets what he wants. In that regard he's exactly like my father. Without backup, she doesn't have a prayer."

Carson leaned forward. "How can we help?"

Ross took a fortifying breath. "Just keep an eye out. Warn Willy about strangers who aren't the typical tourists asking questions about the ranch. I'd like to see her and Andy enjoy the rest of their vacation."

"And when she leaves here, then what?"

Buck always dug deeper and had just asked the sixty-four million dollar question. It was the one Ross had been asking himself all night.

"I don't know yet." The thought of Kit leaving didn't sit well with him. The only thing to do right now was drive to her cabin and talk to her. He couldn't force her to do anything such as forget her plan to go to Texas. Otherwise he'd be guilty of her father-in-law's sin. All he could do was let her know he was there to help.

The guys exchanged glances. Carson said, "Why don't you tell her we all want to pitch in by lightening her load. We turned this place into the daddy dude ranch for that very reason. Andy has lost his father and needs his mother. Those two should be allowed to live their lives as they see fit. That's what our letter to her was all about, right?"

Buck coughed before he stared at Carson. "You just took the words out of my mouth and said them more eloquently than I ever could." He turned to Ross. "No matter who might be coming to look for her, she and Andy should have no worries about staying on the ranch. You tell her that for us. If she's still hesitant, we'll talk to her in person. Between the three of us, we'll keep Andy guarded and entertained."

Ross swallowed hard as he eyed his friends. "You're the best of the best. I knew it in the hospital and know it even more now." He checked his watch. It was seven-thirty in the morning. "Got to run. I'll tell you how the meeting goes with Mac Dawson. He's the oil engineer who'll be meeting me later."

"Sounds good," Carson said.

Buck stood up. "Tell Andy I'll take him and his mom fishing with the Randall and Smoot families as soon as they eat. I'll have them back before Alex and Tracy leave."

"Will do. Thanks."

He left the office, grabbed a couple of donuts from the kitchen and raced out to the truck. Much as he wanted to phone Kit, he couldn't. Ross didn't know her cell phone number. With her and Andy sleeping in the same room, he didn't want to use the house phone or it could awaken them if they were still asleep. The only thing to do was go to the cabin and wait for her.

At seven-forty on the nose he pulled up in front. Instead of sitting in the truck, he climbed out and walked up to the porch, hoping to hear voices through the door. If they were up, then he'd knock. To his surprise, it opened before he had to do anything.

"Hey, Ross—" Andy was wearing his boots and hat. He looked happy. That was good.

"Hey, yourself." They high-fived each other. Kit stood right behind her son. Their eyes met.

"Good morning, Kit. I came to drive you two to breakfast."

"WE WERE JUST about to walk over." Kit knew she sounded a little breathless. But for Ross to be standing there in his cowboy hat, bigger than life and smelling wonderful, her heart thudded so loud she was sure he could hear it.

She could sense from his demeanor he had a special reason for showing up unannounced. Maybe he'd heard from her father-in-law again. Her stomach clenched because it was too soon after her own conversation with Charles. It would probably take years before Kit stopped reacting like that when she thought of him.

"I'd say this was perfect timing," he murmured. "After you eat, Buck is going to take you fly fishing while the trout are biting. He'll have you back in time to go to town with everyone if that's what you want to do."

"What are you going to do this morning?" Andy wanted to know.

"I have a business meeting scheduled out on the property."

"Oh."

OFFICIAL OPINION POLL

Dear Reader,

Since you are a book enthusiast, we would like to know what you think.

Inside you will find a short Opinion Poll. Please participate in our Poll by sharing your opinion on 3 subjects that are very important to all of us.

To thank you for your participation, we would like to send you **2 FREE BOOKS** and **2 FREE GIFTS!**

Please enjoy them with our compliments.

Sincerely,

Pam Powers

YOUR OPINION POLL
THANK-YOU FREE GIFTS INCLUDE:

▶ **2 HARLEQUIN® AMERICAN ROMANCE® BOOKS**
▶ **2 LOVELY SURPRISE GIFTS**

◀ DETACH AND MAIL CARD TODAY! ▶

OFFICIAL OPINION POLL

YOUR OPINION COUNTS!
Please check TRUE or FALSE below to express your opinion about the following statements:

Q1 Do you believe in "true love"?

"TRUE LOVE HAPPENS ONLY ONCE IN A LIFETIME."
○ TRUE
○ FALSE

Q2 Do you think marriage has any value in today's world?

"YOU CAN BE TOTALLY COMMITTED TO SOMEONE WITHOUT BEING MARRIED."
○ TRUE
○ FALSE

Q3 What kind of books do you enjoy?

"A GREAT NOVEL MUST HAVE A HAPPY ENDING."
○ TRUE
○ FALSE

YES! I have placed my sticker in the space provided below. Please send me the **2 FREE books** and **2 FREE gifts** for which I qualify. I understand that I am under no obligation to purchase anything further, as explained on the back of this card.

154/354 HDL F4XP

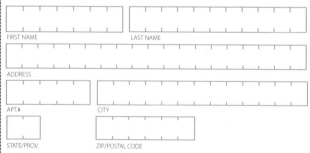

FIRST NAME

LAST NAME

ADDRESS

APT.#

CITY

STATE/PROV.

ZIP/POSTAL CODE

HAR-TF-10/13

Printed in the U.S.A. © 2013 HARLEQUIN ENTERPRISES LIMITED.
® and ™ are trademarks owned and used by the trademark owner and/or its licensee.

⬥ HARLEQUIN® READER SERVICE—Here's How It Works:

Accepting your 2 free books and 2 free gifts (gifts valued at approximately $10.00) places you under no obligation to buy anything. You may keep the books and gifts and return the shipping statement marked "cancel." If you do not cancel, about a month later we'll send you 4 additional books and bill you just $4.74 each in the U.S. or $5.24 each in Canada. That is a savings of at least 14% off the cover price. It's quite a bargain! Shipping and handling is just 50¢ per book in the U.S. and 75¢ per book in Canada.* You may cancel at any time, but if you choose to continue, every month we'll send you 4 more books, which you may either purchase at the discount price or return to us and cancel your subscription.

*Terms and prices subject to change without notice. Prices do not include applicable taxes. Sales tax applicable in N.Y. Canadian residents will be charged applicable taxes. Offer not valid in Quebec. Books received may not be as shown. All orders subject to credit approval. Credit or debit balances in a customer's account(s) may be offset by any other outstanding balance owed by or to the customer. Please allow 4 to 6 weeks for delivery. Offer available while quantities last.

BUSINESS REPLY MAIL

FIRST-CLASS MAIL   PERMIT NO. 717   BUFFALO, NY

POSTAGE WILL BE PAID BY ADDRESSEE

HARLEQUIN READER SERVICE

PO BOX 1341

BUFFALO NY 14240-8571

NO POSTAGE
NECESSARY
IF MAILED
IN THE
UNITED STATES

If offer card is missing write to: Harlequin Reader Service, P.O. Box 1867, Buffalo NY 14240-1867 or visit: www.ReaderService.com

Kit shut the door of the cabin, concerned that her son would become a nuisance if he kept this up. But she had to admit she was curious, too. Everything about Ross fascinated her.

She watched Andy run to the truck and climb over the tailgate as if he'd been doing it all his life. Ross helped her into the cab. Every accidental touch sent delicious sensations through her body. She was pathetic.

"We need to talk," he said after he got behind the wheel.

Kit was bursting with her own news about her talk with Andy. "He can start breakfast without me. Hopefully one of the kids will be there. Have you had another phone call from Charles?" She thought it best to get straight to the point.

His dark brown gaze searched her eyes intently. "No. I came to find out if you had that talk with your son."

Her eyelids smarted. "Yes. He doesn't want to live with them anymore. Andy getting that off his chest was liberating for both of us."

"Thank God for that." He started the engine and they took off.

"You'll never know how happy it has made me. Andy was so sweet. He's carried a terrible burden. The fear of going away to that school must have been torturing him all year. I should have done something about this sooner."

"The important thing is that you're doing it now."

"I know. But right after our talk, my in-laws phoned."

"And?"

"I—I had it out with them." Her voice caught. "It wasn't pretty, but I told them we wouldn't be flying back to Maine after we left the ranch. I didn't tell them where we'd be going, but I promised them I'd keep in touch. And after we were settled, I explained we could all visit each other the way other families do who live apart."

"What happened?"

"Charles hung up on me and Florence broke down sobbing, too incoherent to keep talking."

Ross reached out and grasped her hand. His warmth traveled up her arm to fill her body. "That took a lot of courage, Kit. I want you to know my partners and I are here to support you every way we can."

By now they'd reached the parking area, and Ross pulled into a free space, forcing him to relinquish her hand.

He didn't do it any too soon because Andy had jumped down and come around to her side. The window was already open.

"Honey? I need to talk to Ross. Do you mind going in first? I think you'll find Jenny in there with her dad. We'll join you in a few minutes."

"Okay."

Once he'd disappeared around the corner of the ranch house, she turned to Ross. "I was about to say that your offer of support is very generous, but as I told you last night, my problems aren't your concern."

"They are if your father-in-law decides to fly here and confront you."

"He probably will come, but I'll handle him. I've been doing it for years."

He grimaced. "Except that you've never threatened to move away before. I happen to know Charles Wentworth can be a formidable man when provoked."

She frowned. "How do you know so much about him?"

His sudden smile turned him into the most attractive male she'd ever met in her life. "Allow me to introduce myself fully, *ma'am*." Suddenly he was speaking with a heavy Texas accent.

"My legal name is Rutherford Livingston V, son of Chauncey Livingston IV, son of Ramsey Livingston III, son of Homer Livingston II, son of Eli Livingston, of Livingston Oil of Texas."

Kit blinked in disbelief. Ross was *that* Livingston? The fabulously wealthy U.S. senator she'd heard her husband and father-in-law talk about with envy was Ross's father?

"I can tell by the look on your face you've heard of us," Ross said quietly, leaving off the accent. "The East Coast might have its blue bloods, but so does Houston, the province of the billionaire Livingston oil barons dating from 1900 with their mansions built in River Oaks and Galveston's Historic District. It would seem the divine right of kings is still alive and doing well in both Maine and Texas."

Shocked by the revelation, she was trying to take it all in. "But you're a rancher!"

"I'm working on it. After I was discharged from the service, I couldn't get away from that old life fast enough."

"Ross..."

"Through my mother, who does her share of philanthropy, I've heard of the Wentworth charities run by the women in that family. But I had no idea Kathryn Wentworth was such a beautiful woman until we met at the airport."

"That explains your behavior when I asked you your name. You expected to meet a spoiled, filthy rich society snob without a brain in my head."

His eyes traveled over her. "But we know you're not anything like that!"

"I'm relieved you've revised your opinion of me."

"Forgive me if you sensed any reaction from me. Whatever you assumed I was thinking, I promise it wasn't aimed at you personally. Just so you know, I approve wholeheartedly of giving to charity. If it were up to me, I'd give it all away. But I'm afraid I grew up in the same lifestyle as your husband, and the pall it leaves on the family still sickens me to think about."

Ross was such an extraordinary man, Kit could scarcely comprehend it. She took a deep breath. "Does that mean this ranch is one of your investments?"

"On the contrary," he drawled. "This is Lundgren land since Carson's great great grandfather purchased it in 1908. I'm just lucky enough to be working here."

Kit stared out the window, waiting for the world she'd been living in a minute ago to orbit back to its normal place in the universe. "But you don't have to be here."

"No. I *want* to live and work here. If all goes well, we hope to bring more war widows with their children out here next summer and the summer after that."

"You and your partners have been doing a wonderful thing for three children I know of, Andy in particular."

"I'm glad he's enjoying it, since I'm the one person who probably understands better than anyone else what your life has been like living with Charles Wentworth.

Let me tell you a story about the time I ran away from my family dynasty for good and never looked back."

"*You* ran away?" she blurted. "But your family is worth billions. Wouldn't they have prevented you from leaving?"

"If my father could have done it, he would have, but there was someone even richer and more powerful to stop him."

"I can't imagine who that would be."

"Uncle Sam."

Kit gasped in surprise. With anyone else, she would have thought this was a huge joke, but that wasn't the case with this unbelievable man. "You joined the marines to get away?"

He shot her a dark sideward glance. "Yup. Can you think of a better place to be where my father was powerless to order me back to the Livingston empire? Where his minions couldn't lay a finger on me?"

She let out a sigh. "As a plan, I have to concede it was brilliant." She was beginning to wonder if Winn might have done the same thing to get away from his autocratic father for long periods of time. Andy's comment that his father was afraid of Charles could account for Winn's decision to join the military. Marrying her had been out of character for Winn, yet he'd done it. And they'd all paid a huge price for it.

To her despair, that choice had deprived Andy of a father's love for those same barren periods when Charles had ruled her and his grandson with an iron hand.

"One day during my second year at Harvard Law School, I was sitting in a lecture when I realized I had no idea who I was or what I wanted from life. Like

Andy, I'd been told what, where, when and how to live from the day I was born. I was a robot."

"That's exactly what Charles is turning my son into," she whispered.

"No one can relate better than I can. I had to go to one of those elite, astronomically expensive, pre-adolescent prep schools in Houston when I was nine years old, too. It was called St. Luke's."

Kit sat spellbound as she listened to him tell her the story of his life. The parallel between his and Andy's experiences was uncannily similar.

"Before the end of the lecture one day in class, I had an epiphany. The professor had been discussing a law case that involved a military man. That word military lit up my brain like a neon sign.

"I figured out how to turn my back on my birthright for a nobler cause than helping my family get richer and richer. I would join the marines, not as officer Rutherford Livingston V with all the accompanying perks, but as Ross Livingston, an enlisted man, the same as every other enlisted guy. I wanted no perks.

"That very day I left class and went to the recruiting station to sign up. Once I put my signature on the dotted line, I was untouchable."

She shook her head. "What a shock that must have been to your parents."

"I'm sure it was. Probably no more of a shock than the one you delivered to your in-laws this morning. But when they received my letter, I wasn't there to see it. For the first time in twenty-three years I was free to find out who I was, and my father couldn't do a damn thing about it.

"Being a politician and one of Houston's leading oil tycoons, my father couldn't say anything negative about my choice. Otherwise it would get leaked to the press and possibly ruin his career with all the military voters in his constituency."

"I'm imagining he wanted you to go into politics, too."

"Oh, yes. His aspirations were for me to become President of the United States. He had an agenda all mapped out for me, but of course those were all *his* dreams, and mother was right there with him."

"How awful, Ross. Were you an only child?"

"No. Like your husband, I have two siblings, an elder brother and a younger sister who march to my father's drum and breathe when he breathes. The only real difference between me and Andy is that he's a grandson, not a son. Charles Wentworth got his chance to run your husband's life. That ought to be enough for any man."

She gripped the side of the seat. "I agree."

"Since I made my choice to go into the military, I've been able to love my family much better from a distance." He flashed her a piercing regard. "I applaud you for helping Andy get away before it's too late."

"The thought of my son being sent to a school like yours tears me apart." She bit her lip. "How many years did you have to go to St. Luke's?"

"Four. I hated being away from home. Then I was shipped off to the poshest prep school in the state. By the time I was sixteen, I'd learned to despise the name of Rutherford Livingston V. It was so pretentious I told everyone my name was Ross, after my grandmother Ross."

"Was she a favorite of yours?"

"Yes. When she died, I lost a real friend."

"I know how that feels. I lost mine. It took me years to get over it."

"Some things you don't get over. It didn't take long for me to understand we were one of the wealthiest oil families in Texas. After the Spindletop oil discovery in Beaumont, our great great grandfather joined with other men to form Texas Oil and everything took off. Just belonging to our family made me different from all the other guys I wanted to be my friends.

"I was sent to the best schools, associated with the best people, had the best education in mining engineering at Stanford, vacationed at the best places around the world. All of that to ensure I'd graduate from Harvard Law School before I worked for the family ensuring we amassed more oil. But after two years in, I couldn't do it anymore.

"Like you, I did a lot of reading on my own. By then I'd developed a social conscience.

"Though I'd done everything the folks had wanted for me, it wasn't what *I* wanted. Because I didn't earn any of it, I felt ashamed of all the money we have when millions of people around the world are starving.

"Money opens doors that are closed to people with ordinary incomes or no incomes at all. It made me doubt if the friends and girlfriends I did make were sincere or did they just want something from me. There was a woman my father wanted me to marry named Amanda Hopkins. I liked her, but at the age of twenty-three, I had no clue who I really was.

"Don't get me wrong. I can see the pained look on

your face. I'm not attacking my parents or my lineage that made us who we are. I love them and my brother and sister and always will, but I don't like the trappings."

"Trappings don't bring happiness," she whispered.

"No, just as Andy has found out." He coughed. "By law school I wanted to find out who I really was. I yearned to be an ordinary guy. I wanted to fall in love with an ordinary girl who would fall in love with me. That's why I left school and joined the marines. They call it the great equalizer."

She couldn't take her eyes off him. "Have you found out who you are yet?"

He rubbed the back of his neck. "I'm getting there. Buck and Carson are my *real* friends. There's nothing fake about them. They've never tried to use me and never would. As I've told you, my father is a political animal.

"Naturally I want Dad to win re-election in November because he's a decent man with a lot of great plans, but I don't want to be a part of them. For me to feel good about myself, I've got to make it on my own.

"When I left school, I told him I wanted to serve our country, and nothing could persuade me otherwise. He couldn't argue with that because it was for a good cause." He coughed again.

"But the truth is, I've found my life's work here on the ranch. One day I'll invite the folks here. Seeing how I live will say everything better than words ever could.

"After telling you all this, perhaps now you'll understand why the guys and I want to help you get on with your life. We talked over your problem this morning and are here for you should you run into any real trouble with your father-in-law."

She tried to breathe normally but couldn't. Kit couldn't stand for these wonderful men to be involved in her troubles. She shouldn't have come to the ranch. But if she hadn't, she might never have found the resolve to make the break.

"I feel honored that you would confide in me this way. Thank you for helping me find the strength to do this. And, please, thank your partners for their concern, but I'm sure it won't come to that."

"For yours and Andy's sake, I hope not."

His comment haunted her as she got out of the cab and hurried inside the ranch house dining room to join her son. When she couldn't find him she went into the games room and discovered him playing Ping-Pong with a boy who looked about twelve.

"Hi, Mom. This is Jayce."

"Hello, Jayce."

"Hi."

"He's staying in one of the cabins with his parents."

"That's great. Have you eaten, honey?"

"Yeah."

"Ross and I took a little longer than I thought we would. I'm sorry."

"That's okay."

"I'll be in the dining room when you're through playing."

"Okay."

She retraced her steps and found Ross waiting for her at one of the empty tables.

"Everything all right?"

"Yes. He's already eaten and found a new friend named Jayce. There were quite a few kids on the cruise in Norway, but Andy never played with them. He's so different here, I hardly recognize him."

The waitress brought coffee and took their orders. After she went off Ross said, "That's because the source of his tension is gone. Now that he knows he doesn't have to go back to the mansion to live, you're going to see a new boy.

"I used to be like him until I got completely away from my parents. That's when everything changed. Given his freedom, Andy's going to grow up a happy man."

Their eyes met. "That's what I want for him."

"With a mother like you, he's on his way."

Ross hadn't heard what Florence had said to her earlier. *But you have no skills, no resources. Nothing. How can you possibly care for our grandson?* Those words had pierced her, but the sting was gone. That was because of Ross's faith in her.

How was it that this marvelous man had been here all this time waiting like some guardian angel assigned to watch over them the second they arrived? But she had to remember that an angel was a mortal's friend, not a potential lover.

Kit might want him the way a woman wanted the man she was crazy about, but she was a fool to be thinking of him that way. Not only was he out of her league on every level, she didn't want a man in her life. Winn and Charles had been enough.

Before long their food arrived, and Andy joined them. Ross offered him a piece of bacon, which he ate.

Their behavior was so natural with each other. "Your mom told me you met one of our guests?"

"Yeah. Jayce is from Minnesota. He likes my cowboy hat and said he's going to get his mom to buy him one like it."

Ross smiled at him. "I told you it suited you." Andy beamed. Her son was coming to life being around Ross. "Buck ought to be here by now to take you fishing. Maybe he'll take Jayce with you."

"No. He and his family are going on a float trip with Carson. Do you have to leave for your meeting now?"

Kit blinked in surprise at his question.

"That's right."

"In the truck?"

"Andy—"

"Yes. Why do you want to know?" he asked, ignoring Kit's exclamation.

"I just wondered if I could ride in the back. I won't bother you. I'd rather do that than go fishing."

"You would? Well, I can tell you now I'd like the company." Ross's brown eyes found hers. There was a glint in them that made her feel feverish. "Do you want to come with us? I'm driving to the eastern part of the ranch. There's beautiful scenery along the way."

"But you're going there on business."

"If it's possible, I always mix business with pleasure."

Pleasure. That's what it was like being with Ross. "Andy and I would love to ride out with you." She shouldn't have said it, but this morning she was so happy and felt so free, there was nothing she'd rather do than be with him.

"There's only one problem, Andy. We might not get back in time for you to go into town with the kids."

"I'd rather go with you."

Andy had taken the words right out of Kit's mouth. "Then I'll ring Alex and let her know there's been a change in plans. She'll tell Buck. Do you two need to get anything before we leave?"

"No, but maybe we ought to take a trip to the restroom. Come on, Andy."

"While you do that, I'll get one of the cooks to pack us a lunch. We'll meet at the truck in ten minutes."

After refreshing themselves, Kit and Andy started walking out to the truck. Her son was the one who jumped when her cell phone rang. "It's probably Grandfather."

Kit pulled it out of her pocket and discovered it was her sister-in-law calling. That meant the whole family knew everything. "It's your aunt Corinne."

"I bet he's right there and is making her call you. He always makes her do stuff."

Andy was nobody's fool. "I'm sure you're right." Charles had guilted the whole family to death for years.

"Don't answer it."

"I won't."

He gave her a hug before climbing in the back of the truck. Kit got in the front seat and shut the door. Pretty soon another call came through from Sybil. She let it ring. When everything went silent she checked the message from Corinne.

I can't believe you've done this to my parents after they took you in. Winston did everything conceivable so you could live the enchanted life, and this is how you've repaid him?

Can't you understand the family is worried for Andrew? If you really love him, you'll come home.

Kit stared into space. As far as Corinne was capable of understanding, given the family she'd been born into, she meant well. Neither she nor Sybil could comprehend leaving the gilded nest to go out in the world with their children. But Kit hadn't been born a Wentworth. She was anxious for Andy to have a taste of freedom so he could grow into whatever person he wanted to be.

Her thoughts wandered to Ross who'd said he'd left home in order to find out who he was. As far as she was concerned, it had been the making of a fabulous man who had his feet firmly planted on this ranch. She could only hope the same thing happened to Andy, that he'd find himself and fulfill his potential.

Kit looked through the rear window. He was in the back of the truck shooting off his cap gun like any happy kid. No matter how much guilt the family heaped on her, she wouldn't trade this child for the sullen shadow of himself her boy had been since Winn's death.

Chapter Seven

While he waited for one of the cooks to fill the picnic hamper, Ross took the time to inform the guys he was taking Kit and Andy with him for the day. He also told them to be on the alert now that Kit had let her in-laws know she and Andy were moving out of the mansion.

After stopping in the office for his notebook and a map, he headed for the truck in better spirits than he'd felt in months. His life suddenly seemed filled with new purpose. As he reached the parking area, Andy waved to him from the back.

He walked up and put the hamper in next to one of the hay bales. "You know what, sport? I'm going to swing by your cabin so you can get a sweater or jacket. If you're going to ride back here, it might get a little cool in the forest."

"I'm okay. The sun's really warm right now. If it gets cooler, I'll get in the cab with Mom."

That made sense. "Good enough." On impulse Ross handed him the map. "Have you ever seen a U.S. geological survey map before?"

"No."

He opened it up. "As you can see, it's different from a road map. We're here." He used his index finger to show him the exact location. "We're going to drive over here. This tells you the names and elevations of the land. If you follow it, you'll find it pretty interesting."

"Thanks."

"You're welcome. Holler if you need anything."

"Okay."

"You're sure you don't mind us coming with you?" Kit asked as he got behind the wheel and put his notebook on the backseat. "I'm sorry Andy didn't want to go fishing. I guess you realize it's because you had something else to do. He has a slight case of hero worship at the moment."

He darted her a glance once they'd driven away. "The whole idea of our project is for kids like Andy to open up and express what they want to do. I'm pleased to think he's starting to warm up and feel comfortable."

"You've given him so much attention, I think he's too comfortable. I was watching out the back window. What did you give him to look at?"

"A map so he can see where we're going."

"You're very thoughtful," she said. "What kind of business meeting is it, if you don't mind my asking?"

"Not at all." He had to cough. He hadn't shared his interests with a woman like this in years and loved it. "It's my opinion Carson's ranch is sitting on top of a pocket of natural gas, but we won't know until we drill. I've been doing the research and have received bids from several oil companies. Today I'm meeting one of the engineers from a local firm at the site where I think we should put in a well. If we're lucky, it'll pay big dividends."

He felt her studying him. "We?"

"I graduated as a petroleum engineer before I went to Harvard. Family business, what else?"

She flashed him a brief smile.

"Ranching with Carson has taught me it's a very tough business and money is always tight. I'm hoping a well like this will produce enough natural gas to help him and his family financially for years to come."

"Won't that require a good amount of capital just to get started?"

Kit wasn't just a beautiful face. "Yes. I invested the money I made in the military. It'll be my contribution to our partnership. Carson has already provided the land, and Buck takes care of any construction. Now it's my turn to see what I can do to carry my weight around here."

"But what if the well doesn't produce anything?" she asked. "You'll have lost the investment you took all those years in the military to build up."

"It's a risk I'm willing to take for a friend."

Her eyes darkened with emotion. "The world could use more friends like you. I'm in awe of you, Ross."

"No more than I am of you."

"What do I have to do with anything?"

"For the sake of your son's happiness, you're planning to head out into the unknown on faith and no backing."

"Be serious. My situation isn't the same thing."

They'd been weaving in and out of the forest area and were almost to the flat section of land where he'd ridden with Carson on Saturday morning.

"You're right. I at least have a job as a rancher if my plan fails."

She shook her head. "If my plan to open a bookshop doesn't materialize, I'll get a job right away doing any number of things. But you'll be out hard-earned money."

"I'll live. My concern is how *you're* going to live."

"We'll be fine. That is, if Andy can handle it. If not, we'll go someplace else."

While he pondered her brave words, he heard her cell phone ring. She pulled it out of her pocket and looked at the caller ID, but she didn't answer it. No doubt Charles was harassing her again. The second time it started ringing he heard a muffled sound come out of her. "I'm sorry. I'll turn the ringer off."

"Your father-in-law?"

"No. Now it's my sister-in-law Sybil. Corinne called earlier and left a message. They're both upset with me."

Kit had said she didn't have anyone in her family she could turn to. "Do you want to talk about it?"

"Thanks, but there's really nothing to say. When Charles gets angry, it affects all of them. They just want me to bring Andy home, so the trouble will go away. They know how he and Florence dote on him."

"Have you ever talked to them about the reason why you want to get a place of your own?"

She took a deep breath. "If I ever brought it up before Winn's death, they told me I was crazy. They have lovely homes, but they'd both rather live at the mansion with their children and be pampered. I would have traded places with them in an instant, but they brushed me off.

"I know they think me ungrateful and undeserving, but they've never stopped to consider Andy. Long ago I decided they were jealous that Winn and I could live there. In fact, I know they were jealous of him. It's been very sad, but there was nothing to be done about Charles always showing his preference for Winn."

"Tell me about it," Ross groaned. "My father doted on me. It didn't bother my sister, but my brother has always had a hard time with it. What do you say we change the subject and enjoy the day?" He was getting to the point where he needed to take her in his arms and satisfy this longing for her.

"I'd love to."

Past the trees now, they drove into full sunshine. In the distance Ross could see the oil company truck coming toward them from the road in the opposite direction. "Good. He's right on time."

"I'll keep Andy in the truck."

"You're welcome to get out and join me. This won't take long."

He pulled to a stop. After grabbing his notebook, he climbed out to help her, needing any excuse to touch her. Andy jumped down, and the three of them approached the man getting out of his truck. "Mr. Dawson?"

"You must be Mr. Livingston." They shook hands. His admiring gaze swept over Kit. "Mrs. Livingston? Nice to meet you, too."

"This is Mrs. Wentworth and her son, Andy," Ross corrected him. But the comment wasn't far from Ross's true thoughts. "They're guests on the ranch and wanted to come on the ride to see the property."

The man looked embarrassed. "Sorry about that. My wife tells me I should keep my thoughts to myself. I

guess I assumed because you were riding in the truck
that—"

"It's a natural mistake, Mr. Dawson," Kit cut in with
a smile. "We don't mind, do we?" She hugged Andy,
who shook his head. "I just found out Ross is an oil engineer and is thinking of having a well drilled here."

"You are?" Andy looked up at Ross with renewed
interest. "How soon are you going to do it?"

"Hopefully soon, depending on my partners."

Mr. Dawson nodded. "With all the natural gas in
Wyoming, my instincts tell me it's a pretty sure thing."

"I hope you start before we leave the ranch. I want
to watch."

Ross chuckled. For a minute there, Andy reminded
him of Johnny who was always curious about everything.

"Come on, honey. Let's take a walk so the men can
talk business. Nice to meet you, Mr. Dawson."

"The pleasure's all mine."

Her eyes swerved to Ross a brief moment before she
walked away. He watched her, mesmerized by the mold
of her body. He enjoyed everything about her. Somehow in the past three days he felt she and her son had
become a part of him.

ANDY RAN AHEAD of her to get the map out of the back.
Before they climbed in the truck, he opened it for her.
"Look, Mom. We're right here. This is a lot cooler than
a regular map."

"I agree. It's like a picture of the earth itself."

"Ross knows so much neat stuff. I wish we didn't
have to go to Texas."

It was his first admission that told her he was nervous about their plans and preferred to stay here. "You don't even know what Galveston is like, honey. It'll be exciting. Nila likes you so much, and you and Kim are friends. You can go to school with her. It'll be a place for us to get a new start."

"But what if we don't like it?"

She understood his fears and couldn't afford to ignore them. "Then we'll find another place to work and live."

"Maybe we could come back here."

"No, honey. This is a dude ranch. Once our trip is over, we have to leave."

"I know. I didn't mean the ranch. I meant Jackson."

Jackson? Kit hadn't realized her son had done this much thinking. "We could live there and you could find a job. I could go to school with Johnny and Jenny."

She needed to keep her wits about her. "You're only saying that because these retired marines have become your friends and have shown you such a wonderful time. But they have their own busy lives. We'll make new friends. You'll see."

"But I like Jackson."

"You've only been there twice."

He liked Ross. The man exuded confidence and made both of them feel protected. Already she could tell he felt a bond with the vet who instilled an intangible sense of safety. Kit felt it, too, which was one of the reasons it was equally hard for her to think of leaving.

She could feel Andy getting upset. "Tell you what. Let's enjoy our vacation and then fly to Galveston. If we really don't think it's going to work there, then we'll talk about other possibilities."

"Promise?"

"Promise. Now, not a word to Ross. It looks like the men have finished their meeting. Let's get in the truck."

She quickly climbed in the front while Andy hopped in the backseat. Ross strode toward them on his long, hard-muscled legs. The sight of him never failed to thrill her.

"What do you two say we find ourselves a pretty spot and eat our picnic?" He levered himself in the truck, and they drove back into the forest. At a bifurcation, he took the upper road and they climbed into an area of tall, dark pines that grew close together.

"This is incredible, almost like we're in a green cathedral."

"It'll get even more beautiful in a minute."

Soon they came out in a small clearing of a lush meadow of wild flowers where she could see layers of pines beyond, each layer a different hue of green that went on and on. "What are those flowers?"

"Gentians and Indian paintbrush."

If she looked in the opposite direction, there were the majestic Tetons in all their glory. "The beauty of this defies description," she whispered in awe.

"I think so, too. That's why I thought you'd like to eat here."

"I'd like to live here," her son piped up, echoing her own sentiments.

"I'll let you in on a secret, Andy. This is the spot where I'm going to have Buck build my house. But don't tell anyone yet."

"How come?"

"Because he's still building a house for his new family. When it's done, then I'll talk to him about it."

"Okay. I won't say anything. You sure are lucky. What's it going to be like?"

"An alpine cabin, small and cozy."

Kit could picture it. When she and Andy were in Texas, she'd remember this day and this man....

Ross got out and handed him a thermal blanket from the back of the truck. "Put it anywhere you want."

"Okay." Her son found a spot and she helped him spread it out. Ross brought the hamper. Soon they were munching on sandwiches and salad. He handed them a soda and they sprawled on the blanket, basking in the sun.

Andy reached for more potato chips. "You know that flat place where you're going to drill?"

"Yes?" Ross had just finished off a second sandwich before coughing.

"It's not very far from here, but you can't even see it."

"Nope. That's the beauty of its location. It's out of the way. If the well is a producer, it'll be great news for Carson."

"How do you drill?"

"It's quite a process. A lot of different trucks come. One with pipes, another carries a cable, three others are pump trucks. There's a detergent truck—"

Kit stopped chewing. "Detergent?"

His dark brown gaze fell on her. "That's the material fed into the piping made up of water and sand and other chemicals. Once an open hole is made, you drive deep into the earth, hoping to find the gas."

"How deep?" Andy questioned.

"In my estimation, 11,000 feet."

"Are you teasing?"

Ross flashed them a white smile. "Nope. That's where it's lurking if it's there. Hopefully we'll get lucky. Then there'll be gas 24/7, and clients will come to buy it."

"I had no idea how much is involved." Kit was as fascinated as her son.

"Will it make a lot of noise?"

"Not after it's finished, Andy, but you'll hear its continual flow."

"I wish I could see you drill down. Are you going to let Johnny and Jenny watch?"

Amusement lit his eyes. "If I know those two, they'll be over here a lot."

"But what if there isn't any gas?"

"Then we'll close it back up."

"And drill in another place?"

He raised up on one elbow. "No. This ranch shouldn't be spoiled like that. I'll just have to pray this one works."

"I'll pray, too."

"Yeah?" Ross reached over and tousled Andy's hair.

Kit felt a swelling in her throat. "We'll all pray. You and your partners have given so much for so many, both in the war and here. It's time you got something back in return."

For a while they lay on their backs and rested in silence while Andy got up and walked around. In a minute she felt Ross's hand grasp hers. She turned on her side and saw a longing in his eyes that couldn't be mistaken for anything else.

"This is nice, Kit. You have no idea how nice."

"But I do," she said in a tremulous voice.

He rubbed his thumb over the inside of her wrist. "I want to kiss you more than you can imagine. If Andy weren't with us…"

She sat up and reluctantly removed her arm. "It's a good thing he's where I can see him because kissing you wouldn't be a good idea."

"Why not?"

"We both know why. We're ships passing in the night. Nothing else."

His lids narrowed. "Would it surprise you to know I haven't felt this strong an attraction to a woman in years?"

Her heart leaped. "Actually it would. Surrounded by women on the staff and in the Jackson area, let alone all the female guests who come to your ranch, an attractive man like you has ample, nonending opportunities."

"Opportunities, yes. But not the accompanying desire I need to feel to act on them. You want me, too, so don't deny it. I felt your pulse just now. It runs away with you whenever we're together. I see the throbbing in the hollow of your throat, and I want to put my lips to it."

She started putting things away in the hamper. "You're a bachelor and will feel the same way about another woman before long. But I'm not in a position to give into an impulse, especially not with our gracious host. I'm in the most precarious circumstances of my life. One wrong step could jeopardize everything. Andy is so vulnerable right now, it terrifies me."

Ross got to his feet. "I understand that, but the day is coming before you leave when I'm going to give in to my own impulse, so watch out."

No. That day wouldn't be coming. By the end of the week, she and Andy would be flying to Galveston. Much as she hated the idea of leaving here, she needed to be out on her own.

Having been confined at the mansion for too many years by her broken marriage and Charles's domination, she needed freedom from any strings. Getting to know Ross any better would not be in her best interests. Intimacy blurred the lines, making it difficult to focus.

She closed the hamper for him to put in the truck. "Andy?" She waved to her son. "We're leaving. Come on!"

Kit folded the blanket. As she started walking toward Ross, her cell phone rang again. Her gaze automatically flew to his. He stood there with a distinct frown marring his handsome features. It was as if the sound punctuated better than words the instability of her situation. No words passed between them as he put the blanket away.

Andy joined them. "I wish we didn't have to go. I want to hike up higher and see everything."

"There's a lake up above those trees shaped like a sea horse."

"A sea horse?"

Ross chuckled. "Cross my heart. Carson has a picture of it from the air. It's got fish, but you have to work for them. What do you say we plan to come back here tomorrow? We'll hike around and have an overnight campout. Whatever we catch, we'll eat."

"That would be great!"

As far as Kit was concerned, Ross's plans had just made Andy's whole trip for him. He was starving for attention, but the three of them alone for overnight probably wasn't the smartest plan. Better to add to the group.

She put an arm around his shoulders, warm from the sun. "I think it's a terrific idea." Without looking at their host, she said, "If it's all right with Ross, maybe Jenny and Johnny can come."

"The more the merrier," he said at once. "We'll ask them at dinner."

To her relief Andy didn't complain about the other kids coming and got in the backseat. That was another relief. As long as he rode inside the truck with them, she wouldn't be getting into another personal conversation with Ross she couldn't handle.

She hadn't stopped trembling since he'd told her he wanted her. *You want me, too.* The fact that what he'd said was true had really shaken her.

Thankfully Ross and Andy chatted on the way home about fishing and hunting. To her surprise it was already three-thirty when they arrived back. When she was with Ross, the time went by too fast.

Before her son asked Ross what he'd be doing later, Kit asked if he would drop them off at the ranch house. She announced that she wanted to get one of the puzzles from the game room. They'd walk back to the cabin and work on it until dinner. Without looking at him she thanked him for the outing, and they parted company.

"See you at dinner," Andy called to him.

"I'll be there."

ROSS WATCHED THEM round the corner of the ranch house. His ache for Kit had grown. Knowing she wanted him too helped him keep his sanity. Tonight after Andy went to bed, he'd get her alone and end this insufferable hunger.

After returning the hamper to the kitchen, he walked down the hall to the office with his notebook in hand. Now that Ross had met with Mac Dawson, Carson needed to see the recent figures and calculations for the project and give his okay. Ross was crossing his fingers because, like Mac, he had a hunch the natural gas was there waiting.

He entered his notes into the computer, excited for the drilling to get started. Andy's comment that he'd pray the well would produce had touched Ross's heart. He was a sweet boy like Johnny with a depth and intelligence Ross found exceptionally appealing. Andy was Kit's son. That accounted for a big part of it. No one could have a better mother. Naturally he'd inherited some of his father's good qualities, too.

Who would have thought all this had been hidden inside the unhappy boy who'd first arrived here? When Ross thought of his reservations at meeting her and Andy, he was ashamed.

A tap on the door caused his head to lift, bringing him back to the present. "Come on in."

"Boss?" Willy closed the door behind him. "I'm glad you're back. The Teton County Sheriff, Leo Barton, is out in the foyer wanting to speak to you personally about a missing person."

Personally?

Well, well, well. The sheriff, no less. After all those phone calls Kit hadn't answered this morning, Charles Wentworth had wasted no time.

"Do you want me to show him in here?"

"Please." The less drama in front of their guests coming in and out of the ranch house, the better. "Thank you, Willy."

The younger man paused at the door. "What's going on?"

"When I know, you will, too."

His brows lifted. "Okay."

A minute later he heard another knock on the door. Ross got up to open it. "Sheriff Barton? Come in and sit down."

"Thank you, Mr. Livingston."

"How can I help you?"

"Do you have guests staying here by the name of Kathryn Wentworth? She's with a nine-year-old boy named Andrew?"

"Yes, that's her son. They arrived on Saturday. What's wrong?"

"Her in-laws, Mr. and Mrs. Charles Wentworth, have reason to suspect they might have gone missing since then. I have a warrant issued by Judge Otis Marcroft in Knox County, Maine, to look for them."

Good grief.

Ross pretended to be surprised. "You mean the Wentworths think she's been kidnapped while she's been here on the ranch?"

"I can't answer that question. My job is to search the premises for them."

"You don't need to search. I'll take you to them in my truck. I was with them all day until about a half hour ago when I dropped them off. They're in their cabin."

The sheriff scratched his head. "You say you were with them all day?"

"That's right. I've been with them 24/7 since they came to the ranch. Today we were out at the eastern end of the property. I had a meeting with Mac Dawson from the Dawson Gas Company in Jackson. He can vouch for them since I introduced them to him."

"I'd be obliged if you'd show me to their cabin."

"My truck's around the side."

They walked out past a bewildered-looking Willy. Once the sheriff got in beside him, Ross headed for the cabin. He wished he could have prepared Kit and Andy, but his hands were tied. This could be a frightening experience for a young boy whose only fault was to be the grandson of Genghis Khan.

There was something mentally wrong with Charles Wentworth to be willing to scare his grandson like this in order to make Kit cave to his demands.

Over Ross's dead body.

He pulled up and followed the sheriff to the porch. The older man gave a loud knock.

Soon Kit opened the door. Andy was right behind her. He could see the puzzle they'd been working on set up on the table.

The sheriff examined them from head to toe. "Good afternoon, ma'am. I'm Sheriff Barton from the Teton County Sheriff's Office in Jackson. You're Kathryn Wentworth?"

Ross could read Kit's mind. She knew exactly what was going on and lifted her proud chin. He admired her more than anyone he knew for her sheer guts in handling a bad situation.

"I am, and this is my son Andrew Wentworth. How can I help you?"

"I'd like to see your identification, please."

"Just a moment." She went over to the table for her purse and pulled out a wallet. She came back to the door and showed him her driver's license. While he was at it, he looked through her pictures.

Andy had lost a little color, but he stood there at his mother's side like a man. A feeling of love for the boy swept through Ross.

"I was issued a warrant to locate you." He handed her back the wallet.

"By whom?"

"Your father-in-law has been looking for you and was ready to file a missing person's report."

"Be he *knows* I'm here. I don't understand. Andy and I have been on this ranch since the moment we flew in from Bar Harbor on Saturday. We've been in constant telephone contact with Andy's grandparents until today when Mr. Livingston took us sightseeing on the property.

"Check his telephone records and mine. They'll verify we've had several phone calls, sometimes twice a day, proving we've been in contact. Unless someone told him we'd been kidnapped today, Charles has no reason to think anything. At the invitation of the owners of this ranch who made this trip possible for us, Andy and I have been having a marvelous time!"

"Is that true, son?"

"Yup. Ross has shown me the best time ever."

Oh, Andy. The boy's genuineness and innocence stuck out a mile.

Ross had it in his heart to almost feel sorry for the

sheriff who'd been sent on a fool's errand. By the ruddy color that crept into his face, the man knew it.

"How long will you be on the ranch?"

"We leave Saturday."

"And your plans after that?"

"Does that warrant include finding out my future plans? Because if it does, I'm not sure of them yet."

Kit knew what she was doing. She wasn't about to disclose her destination once she left here.

"No, ma'am."

"Then is that all, Sheriff?"

"Yes, ma'am. Sorry to disturb you."

"That's all right." She shut the door, but not before her eyes flicked to Ross with a glimmer of mirth. Kit Wentworth was a prize, packaged with the stuff men's dreams were made of.

He got back in the truck and drove the sheriff to his decked-out police van parked in front where everyone walking around could see it. Their guests had to wonder what was happening. After learning that Charles Wentworth was at the bottom of this warrant, Ross bet he'd driven in here all bells and whistles. He probably hadn't had a mission this exciting in years!

Carson stepped outside from the foyer. No doubt Willy had already told him about the visit. He walked over and tipped his hat. "Sheriff Barton?"

"Carson." They shook hands.

"Haven't seen you in a while. Did you find the people you were looking for?"

"Yup. They were at their cabin."

"Anything else we can do for you?"

"Nope. I have a hell of lot of things more important

to do than come chasing out here for someone who's not missing."

"Oh, well. It's all in a day's work, right?"

He nodded and climbed in his van. "Looks like you're doing a right fine business. Your granddad would be proud of you."

Carson smiled at Ross. "Thanks to my partners here, it's growing. That's for sure. Take care now."

They both watched until the van was out of sight before bursting into laughter. Ross turned to him. "You should have seen Kit after she opened the door. She handled him like a pro. So did Andy."

"To do this in front of Andy, that father-in-law of hers is a real nasty piece of work, Ross."

"You can say that again. I'm going back to the cabin to make sure they're all right."

"Go ahead."

"I take it the kids aren't back yet."

"Tracy called. They just got out of the movie and will be home soon."

"Good. Tomorrow I'm planning to take Andy and Kit on an overnight campout to Bluebell Lake. If the kids could join us, Andy would like it."

"I think we'd all love it! I'll talk to the girls and Buck about it."

"Good."

"Just so you know, I was reading over your notes on the meeting with Dawson when Willy came in the office and told me what was going on. We'll get together later with Buck and talk about it."

"I've got a feeling about this well, Carson."

"Yeah?" His friend's blue eyes darkened with emotion. Ross was glad Carson wasn't going to let his grandfather's reservations prevent them from trying this experiment. If it was successful, he'd be perpetuating the Lundgren legacy far into the future. One day Johnny and any other children they might have would be in charge and it would go on from there. "Your hunch means a hell of a lot."

On that happy note, Ross took off for the cabin. Instead of knocking, he called through the door so they'd know who was on the other side.

Andy flung it open. The concern on his face was too much. Without thinking, Ross pulled him into his arms and gave him a hug. The boy clung to him. "I was proud of the way you handled yourself in front of the sheriff. That took real courage."

"That's what I told him."

Ross saw Kit standing in the background and let go of Andy. "Neither of you should have been forced to go through that experience. If there'd been any other way…" His voice grated. "But since he had a warrant, I couldn't stop him or warn you. He had to come out here and see for himself."

"I know, and believe it or not, I'm not sorry. I've had a lifetime learning experience within the last half hour. Not only did I discover new things about myself, I learned a lot about my son who's much stronger than I'd ever imagined he could be, thanks to your example. And there's something else."

"What's that?"

"Andy, honey? Would you mind going outside for just a minute? I need to talk to Ross in private."

"Okay." He grabbed his cap gun and went out the door.

She shut it and backed up against it. "Andy doesn't know that this morning I listened to Corinne's phone message, and I have to admit it shook me up a little. But no longer. After this experience, I know I'm doing the right thing to move out. There's a cruel streak in Charles. I'm positive Florence is disturbed by it, but long ago she made the choice to stay and support him.

"By sending that sheriff out here, he's committed the ultimate crime against Andy, in my opinion. No child should have to endure what happened today because Charles is upset with me."

"Amen."

Kit took a second breath. "He's done an unconscionable act."

Ross knew he was talking to the most extraordinary woman he'd ever met. For years she'd undergone a form of emotional abuse within the walls of the Wentworth mansion. He couldn't find the words to tell her how pained he was for her ordeal. But she was standing up to Charles. That told Ross what this woman was really made of.

In the next breath his hands shot out on either side of her, trapping her. The heat generated by their bodies worked like an aphrodisiac on Ross. His body moved closer until they were molded to each other.

"*Ross*—no—we mustn't." Her voice came out on a strangled whisper.

"A man can only take so much. I warned you."

He lowered his head and covered her mouth with his own, parting her lips because his hunger was so great. At first she held back, but with each kiss he drove deeper and deeper; she began to succumb until they were giving kiss for kiss.

Her response released an explosion of feeling he could hardly contain. While he was immersed in sensual ecstasy, she wound her arms around his waist, creating greater intimacy. Driven by this mindless passion for her, time ceased to exist.

"You have no idea how beautiful you are to me, Kit. I'm talking inside and out." Their kisses grew more prolonged. Somehow he'd moved so his back was against the door and his legs were cradling hers. Each kiss felt natural. Her soft, sweet body melted into his. He couldn't get enough of her as their mouths clung.

"I want you," he cried, "but you already know that." The feel and taste of her transcended any of his dreams. She was all warmth and beauty. Slowly their kisses grew more urgent. He pressed her closer, running his hands through her hair and over her back.

"I've been so afraid for you to touch me," came her feverish response.

"There's nothing to be afraid of. How could there be?" Growing along with his desire was this powerful need to protect her. Ross wanted to make up to her for the years she'd suffered at the hands of the Wentworth men.

Charles had been so blessed to have a daughter-in-law as sweet as Kit. Since his son's passing, he'd figuratively trampled her beneath his feet and had lost a lot of the love of his grandson in the process. Ross couldn't comprehend it or the sorrow she'd suffered, having lost a spouse who hadn't been there for her. If Kit would let him love her in all the ways she needed to be loved…

"You don't understand. This can't go on—" She tore her lips from his on a moan.

"Why are you pulling away from me?" he asked.

"Because I feel...cheap."

Ross was incredulous. "Do *I* make you feel that way?"

She eyed him with a frazzled look. "Of course not. It's not you."

"Then explain what you mean. You owe me that much."

"I owe you *everything!*" she cried. "That's the problem. I only arrived here last Saturday. Set free from my prison, I've already taken your protection, your good will. I've involved your partners in the ugliness of my life. Andy and I have taken up all your time."

"We invited you here, remember?"

"Yes I remember, but my husband only died ten months ago, and yet I'm here in this cabin making out with you like a high school girl looking for a good time with the first guy to look my way."

"By your own admission you fell out of love years ago. It's a wonder you've taken this long to feel alive again. I'm only thankful it's happened with me because you've made me feel alive again, too."

"But this is wrong."

He needed to understand. "Surely you realize that's your fear talking."

"Yes. I know it is and I'm sorry, Ross. Forgive me for venting," she begged. "I must seem like the most mixed-up, ungrateful wretch who ever lived. Can we just start over again and forget what has happened?"

Ross studied her features. "No. At least *I* can't. To

try to forget would be pointless when I'd be fighting against nature. Would it surprise you to know I wanted to kiss you before I left the cabin the first day?"

Kit smoothed the hair away from her temples. "You didn't even like me."

"You're wrong. I didn't want to like you for the reasons we've already talked about, but I couldn't help myself."

"Now you're simply trying to make me feel better like you always do."

He let out a bark of harsh laughter. "I'm glad to hear that. Don't you know I'm trying to be as honest with you as I can? Here this grieving woman comes to the ranch with her grieving son at our invitation and I find myself desiring you. What does that say about me? So much for my being a saint."

She shook her head. "Don't you see? We shouldn't be spending this much time together alone."

"But we haven't actually been alone until now."

"And look what's happened!"

"Didn't you enjoy it?"

"Yes, but it was a guilty enjoyment I'm not proud of."

"Guilty?" he whispered.

"Yes. Don't ask me to explain."

"Then after I've figured it out, how about we try it again and see if you haven't changed your mind."

She pressed her hands against his chest. "Ross?"

"Yes?" He coughed.

"Please, be serious."

"In other words, try to pretend that you're not a beautiful woman I'd like to get to know better?"

Kit swallowed hard. "You don't want to know me."

"What in the hell does that mean?"

"You deserve a woman who can be your counterpart in every way. If we'd met under ordinary circumstances, you would have gotten your full measure of me in about two minutes and passed on by."

"Two minutes? You don't give yourself any credit, or me for having discernment."

"You're just being a gentleman. That's the trouble with you. I'll never get to know the Ross Livingston who lives inside his own skin. You're saving that for the special woman who'll come along one day. That's one of the reasons why it would be wrong for us to get physical because of chemistry alone."

"What's the other reason?"

"Andy and I will be gone soon. I don't want to leave with regrets."

"Do you regret kissing me?"

"Yes."

"I think you actually meant that."

"I do. The fact is, I need a clear head."

"So any intimate involvement with me would muddy the waters?"

"After my past with the Wentworth men, I don't need more complications that will lead nowhere."

She'd pressed on a nerve. "You think having a relationship with me will lead nowhere?"

"I didn't mean that the way it sounded. All I'm saying is, it would be better if we don't start up anything. In a few days I'll be gone. My whole focus needs to be on making a home for Andy and getting on with a career."

On a groan of protest he buried his face in her dark,

luxuriant hair. "A fire's been lit. There's no way we can let each other go. Not now, not ever."

Somewhere in the periphery he heard children's voices and caps firing. "*Mom?* The kids are here. Can we come in?"

"Ross—we have to stop!" Kit sounded frantic.

He pressed another hot kiss to her mouth before finally releasing her and taking a step away. "Only for now," he vowed and staggered his way over to the fridge. He opened a can of pop while he tried to get himself under some semblance of control.

One look at Kit and he saw she was having the same problem. She rushed into the bathroom and shut the door.

"Come on in, guys!" he called to the children and opened the front door.

Johnny was the first inside. "Daddy told us we're going on a campout tomorrow."

Ross stood there with his hands on his hips, still shaken by the desire he felt for her. "What's this? No hello first?"

Jenny came inside with Andy. "Hi, Uncle Ross."

"That's more like it. Hi, yourself! Did you guys have fun at the movie?"

"Yes. Are we going to Secret Lake?"

His laugh brought on a cough. That was the kids' favorite place on the ranch so far and the first thing on their minds. "Nope. We're going to one you've never seen before."

"Huh?" Johnny looked shocked. "Another lake?"

"It looks like a sea horse," Andy spoke up.

"Andy's right," he said when he saw the other children's surprised expressions. "Carson calls it Bluebell Lake because of the wild bluebells that grow near the tail. Since we're going to be doing some hiking, we won't be taking the ponies this time. We'll go up in the truck and set up camp."

"Goody!"

Kit came into the living room. Except for her glazed eyes, she looked composed for someone who'd just been kissed senseless. "I'm so glad to see all of you. You're just in time for us to go to dinner."

Jenny stared up at her. "After we eat, will you read some more to us about Buck?"

"Absolutely. I'm glad you reminded me." She reached for the book on the coffee table.

"Let's go."

"Everybody, pile in the truck!" Ross helped Jenny before he started the engine. Kit put on a good front, but he knew she was quaking inside over what had happened and would never be the same again. *Neither would he.*

Chapter Eight

"Nila? Is this a bad time to call you?" It was nine o'clock at night. Kit and Andy had just gotten back from the ranch house.

"It's a great time. What's going on?"

After Kit had finished the first chapter of the Jack London book for the children, she and Andy had said good-night to everyone and come straight home. While he was in the living room watching TV in his pajamas, she paced the bedroom floor.

"For one thing, the local sheriff paid a visit to my cabin earlier today. Guess who got a court order to make sure I hadn't left Wyoming yet?" She kept no secrets from Nila.

"I'm not surprised. The sooner you get here, the better I'm going to feel."

She gripped the phone tighter. "That's why I'm calling. Ross has arranged an overnight camping trip for tomorrow with the children and—"

"Ross?" Nila broke in.

"Mr. Livingston, one of the partners here on the dude ranch. He's been the one in charge of us."

"Hmm. A retired marine. How old is he?"

"Early thirties I think."

"Tall, dark and handsome?"

"You got it in one."

"You're kidding."

"No. The cliché fits him down to his well-worn cowboy boots."

"Oh, boy."

"Oh, boy is right, but I don't dare talk about him at the moment. Because of this overnight outing, we'll be away from the ranch where Charles won't be able to find us *if* that's on his agenda. That's a good thing. We'll get back sometime Wednesday.

"Since my father-in-law knows my original flight arrangements, which have us flying back to Maine on Saturday, I'm thinking of leaving the ranch on Friday just to throw him off. That is if Andy can handle it. The children he's gotten to know here start school on Thursday and will be in class on Friday, as well. Knowing that, Andy might not mind leaving a day early." Kit knew she was avoiding how Andy would feel about leaving Ross. Never mind her own feelings.

"I've looked at the airline schedules and have booked a flight out to Salt Lake. From there we'll get a connection and be in Galveston at 5:30. I know it's a day earlier than we planned, but I think it's for the best." It was best for Kit. Ross had her so bewitched, she couldn't think clearly. "Don't worry about picking us up. We'll take a taxi to your house."

Andy wouldn't like it, but seeing the writing on the wall with Ross, she realized she needed to get away from him before she broke down and made a mistake she'd never recover from. While they were on the campout, the children would be her buffer. After that she would make certain they did safe activities with Ross until it was time to leave.

"I'm going to pick you up, Kit. Just let me know the time."

"All right. You're the best friend in the world."

"Ditto. How's Andy?"

"As you know, he didn't want to come out here at first, but now he's loving it."

"Something tells me Ross Livingston has a lot to do with his turnaround."

He had everything to do with it.

"Ross and his partners. They and their families have shown Andy such a great time already. He's never had this kind of attention and doesn't want to leave. But he doesn't want to live with his grandparents anymore, so he's willing to see what Galveston is like."

"He's a little trooper. We'll do everything we can here to make him happy. Kim's looking forward to it."

"I am, too. It'll be great seeing you again. Until Friday night, then."

Kit hung up and went back to the living room. Andy was munching on a granola bar. "Aren't you too full from dinner to eat that?"

"No. I just felt like one. They're really good. Do you want a bite?"

"Thank you, but I don't dare eat any more snacks or I'm going to gain weight." Needing to do something with her nervous energy, she sat down at the table to keep working on the puzzle.

With each day Kit noticed more changes in him. A new confidence had taken hold, one she was grateful to see. The shadows and furtive looks seemed to be disappearing. She wanted him to stay like this and dreaded telling him they were leaving Friday. But that could wait until Wednesday evening after they'd returned from their overnight trip.

"Mom? Do you like Ross?"

His question didn't exactly surprise her. She'd known it would come up at some point, just not this soon. "Who wouldn't like him?"

He wandered over to the table to watch her. "Do you think you'll ever get married again?"

She felt a sudden burst of adrenaline. "Where did that question come from?"

"Johnny and Jenny were talking about it while we were playing Ping-Pong after dinner."

"I see." Kit had to force herself not to overreact. "That's because their mothers both got married recently."

"They wish you would marry Ross."

She couldn't help smiling. "They do?"

"Yes. They love Ross and think you are really nice."

"Well, that's nice to hear." Kit believed what her son was telling her, but she also believed Andy was projecting some of his own feelings where Ross was concerned. "You like him a lot, don't you?"

"Will you get mad at me if I tell you the truth?"

She reached out to hug him. "I could never get mad at you for being honest. Not ever."

"Now that my dad is gone, I wish Ross could be my new dad."

Oh, no, Andy.

Kit got up from the table and walked over to the minifridge for a can of cola.

"See? You *are* mad."

"No, honey."

"Yes, you are. You don't want me to like him because of Dad."

She spun around, almost spilling her drink. "That's not true. I know how much you loved your father and always will, but now that he's gone, it doesn't mean you can't learn to love someone else. Ross is a wonderful man, and any boy would be blessed to have him for a father. But in order for that to happen—"

"I know," he broke in before she could finish. "He'd have to love me the way Carson loves Johnny." Sometimes Andy sounded wise beyond his years. Just now the wistfulness in his tone crept into her heart. His gray eyes squinted up at her. "If he asked you, would you marry him? Johnny says Ross really, really likes you."

"Andy—" She shouldn't have taken that second swallow and choked on it. "We hardly know each other!" Insecurity was driving her son to say these things. "It's too soon for me to think about getting married. I want to work and take care of you. That Johnny—he does way too much talking."

"He's funny, Mom."

"I agree, but he sometimes says things he shouldn't."

"That's what Ross says. Did you know his parents got married five weeks after they came to the ranch? Jenny said her parents got married in private after ten days."

Kit put the can on the table. "I know their marriages happened fast." Incredibly fast. It was hard to believe, and yet these retired marines were exceptional men. It was no wonder Alex and Tracy had fallen in love with them.

But for those four people to marry so soon and be sure… Kit had been so sure when she'd married Winn, never realizing the nightmare that awaited her. The thought of going into another marriage where she could be dominated was frightening.

When the house phone rang, she jumped.

"I bet that's Ross!" Andy ran in the bedroom.

"Wait—" She followed, but he was too quick for her and picked up. "Hello?" After a pause, "Hi! Yeah! I'm in my pajamas. Hey, Mom? Can Ross come over and help us with the puzzle? He says he's not tired yet and I'm not either."

Ross had a definite reason for wanting to come over, but she didn't know what it was. As usual he knew how to handle Andy so he wouldn't get alarmed. In fact, her son was thrilled. "If he'd really like to."

Andy repeated her message before he hung up. "He says he's driving over now."

Right or wrong or unwise, he was coming and Kit couldn't do anything about it. With her heart thudding in her chest, she hurried in the bathroom to brush her hair and put on some lipstick.

Before long they heard the knock on the door, and Andy opened it. Ross's gaze darted to her. "Thanks for letting me come. I have the whole top floor of the ranch house to myself. Sometimes it gets lonely."

"My grandparents' mansion felt the same way to me when I had to go to bed."

Andy's comment squeezed her heart. "Well, tonight nobody's lonely."

Ross coughed. "Mind if I help with the puzzle?"

"Be our guest."

The three of them sat down at the table.

"I'm glad I don't have to go away to that school."

"I didn't like the boarding school I went to," Ross interjected. He'd already found some puzzle pieces that fit. "I only got to go home once a month."

"Johnny and Jenny are lucky they get to go to school in Jackson."

"I agree, except they're kind of scared."

"Why?"

"Well, Johnny went to school in Ohio before he came here, and Jenny was in school in California. They don't have any friends yet except each other. It's going to take them a little time to adjust at Snake River Elementary, but they're tough."

Kit suspected Ross was trying to prepare Andy for when they went to Texas.

"That's a funny name for a school."

Ross chuckled. "Speaking of snakes, has Johnny told you about the pet snake he keeps in his room? His name is Fred."

"Fred?" Both of them broke into laughter.

"No one knows why he picked that name. Last month Jenny gave him a T-shirt for his birthday that has a snake on the front. The writing above says 'Fred's Dad.'"

Kit smiled. "That's one shirt I've got to see. He's such a character."

"So's Jenny. She's the one who thought it up and designed it."

"They're both precious."

Andy looked at Ross. "Do you want to see a picture of my dad?"

Kit was stunned. More and more he was opening up around Ross. Already she knew Andy wouldn't want to leave here when the time came.

"I was hoping you'd show one to me."

"I'll get it." He was back in a flash. "Here he is."

Ross took the five-by-seven framed photo from him. "I've seen other pictures of him, but this one is special. He's one fine-looking marine you can be proud of. When you're a man, you're going to look a lot like him."

"Thanks. Did you like being a marine?"

"I learned to like it a lot."

"I don't want to be one. They get killed."

"You're right. Some of them do." His black brows lifted as he looked at Andy. "You know what? That's the great thing about being your own person. You get to do what you want with your own life. What do you think you'd like to be?"

"I've been thinking about that, but I don't know yet."

Kit couldn't believe what she'd just heard. Andy was talking like a grown-up.

"Well, you've got years to find out."

"Do you like being a rancher?"

"I love it, but I didn't know I wanted to be one until Carson invited me to his ranch last March."

"What happened?"

"Well, we got on horses, and he showed me the whole property. I felt like I was seeing country no other man had ever seen or walked on. Each time we came to a different spot, I marveled at the wild beauty of the land and the mountains. I felt like it was calling to me and I had to be a part of it."

Kit got gooseflesh while he described his feelings.

"As we rode, he told me the stories about his ancestors and how they came to settle here. It was such a different world from the one I'd come from, it was like I'd been living on a different planet. I kept thinking a man could live here, put down roots and be happy.

"The truth is, Andy, I'd never truly been happy because I had a dad who expected me to be a certain way all the time."

"Did he die?"

"No. He and my mom live in Houston, Texas, the home of the big oil wells. I have a married brother Scott and a married sister Georgianna, but I call her Georgie Porgie. She doesn't like that." Andy laughed. "I love them a lot, but I have to do my own thing."

"My dad had to do what my grandfather said."

He cocked his head. "But from now on, you and your mom get to do what *you* want. Right?"

"Yeah. Thanks for talking to me."

"Anytime."

Afraid she'd break down bawling if she heard any more, Kit said, "With that settled, it's getting late, honey. We've had a huge day. You need to brush your teeth and get to bed."

"Okay. Good night, Ross."

He handed the picture back to him. "Thanks for showing this to me. Get a good sleep. I'll see you in the morning. We'll pack up and head for Bluebell Lake."

"Yeah!"

Andy gave Kit a hug and left the room. No sooner had he shut the door to the hall than Kit's cell phone rang. Ross shot her a glance.

She reached for it, but for the first time she didn't get

that sick feeling inside. "It's Charles. He never gives up. I'm going to turn off the ringer so I won't be bothered for the rest of the night."

"That sounds like a good idea."

After fixing it, she said, "What's the real reason you came over tonight?"

He lounged back in the chair and extended his long legs. "I'm going to ask you a question, but you don't have to answer it. In fact you can tell me to take a hike."

She chuckled. "I'd never do that."

"I guess we're going to find out if that's true. As I recall, you told me that when you get to Texas, your savings will only keep you for a while. That could mean any number of things. How much money do you really have on hand?"

Kit clasped her hands beneath the table. "It's enough."

"That's what I thought." He got to his feet.

"Where are you going?" she asked jerkily.

"To take that hike."

"I didn't mean to be rude to you."

"I know that. I've asked you something that's none of my business and took the risk because I care what happens to you and Andy. Get a good sleep." He started for the door.

"Don't go yet. Please—"

He stood there rubbing the back of his neck. "I only asked because after ten years of marriage, I would have assumed you had enough money saved to keep you going a lot longer than that."

She let out a small moan. "Nothing about my marriage was conventional. I wasn't allowed to work. That was unheard of for a Wentworth. Since I earned no money, I was dependent on Winn and his father for everything."

Incredulous, he moved closer to her. "So what you're saying is, you had no discretionary income if you wanted to buy something for you or Andy without their approval?"

"That's what I'm saying."

The silence that followed was deafening.

Ross stared down at her, appalled by the revelation. "Where's the money your husband made while he was in the service?"

"Winn's military pay was always funneled into a special investment I couldn't touch."

His dark brown eyes searched hers. "So, how do you have any money at all?"

"At my grandmother's death, she willed me her books and the $3,000 she had in her savings account. I had it invested in a CD money account that grew interest before I met Winn. He didn't know about it. Four days ago I drew out $10,000."

He hooked the leg of the chair and sat down. "Throughout your entire marriage, you had no money that you could actually handle yourself?"

"That's right."

"So without that CD, you'd have nothing?" She felt his quiet anger.

"I know it sounds incredible. Winn and his father did it to prevent me from leaving with Andy. They never knew about my grandmother's money. I never touched it because I knew that one day I'd need it. When your invitation from the ranch came, I decided it was our passport to a new life."

"How did you get access to the money? Wouldn't they know if you went to Point Judith to get it?"

"Yes. When Nila knew about my plans, she came to Bar Harbor on the pretext of visiting her mother and gave me some money to help me. After Andy and I flew from Norway, we landed in Providence, Rhode Island. I rented a car and we drove to the bank in Point Judith where I withdrew my money.

"I asked the bank to write me a cashier's check, then we returned to Providence for the rest of our flight out here. That's one of the reasons Andy was extra tired. The poor guy had to endure too many plane trips in one day."

Her story was so unbelievable, she couldn't have made it up. "You still have that check on you?"

"Yes. I plan to deposit it in a bank in Galveston and pay Nila back."

Lines darkened his features so she hardly recognized him. "I'm still trying to get my head around the fact that you lived ten years at the mercy of your husband's family. How did it work?"

"Between Winn and Charles, they paid for everything I needed."

"And they decided *what* you needed, *when* you needed it?"

At this point Kit stood up. "Yes." She couldn't look at him.

"And you're going to Galveston to start a new life with only $10,000?"

"Minus the $1500 I have to repay Nila for taxi money and our airline tickets. I also have the diamond ring Winn gave me. It's the only piece of jewelry I possess.

It was appraised at $18,000. I plan to sell it when I get there."

His mouth had thinned to a white line. "I'm afraid you won't get half of what it's worth if you try to sell it. There are other benefits that should be coming to you because of his years in the military."

"I know, but I haven't seen them. Charles goes through all the incoming mail first."

Kit heard him suck in his breath. "You need an attorney to bring a lawsuit in order to claim the investments your husband made throughout your marriage. That money, maybe all or a portion of it, is legally yours. Whatever the amount, you need it to help you get established in Texas or anywhere else."

"I can't count on it," she said. "I imagine Winn made an airtight will with his father's help. Any of that money will go to Andy when he comes of age. But Charles has never discussed it with me, nor would he."

By now Ross was on his feet once more. "Were you married in Rhode Island?"

"Yes, in a civil ceremony at the courthouse."

"That might have some bearing on your case. An attorney will know the probate laws for Maine and Rhode Island. Through discovery you'll find out the facts and go from there."

"I can't afford one."

His eyes studied her with an intensity that shook her. "I know an attorney who will take your case. It's the only way for you and Andy to receive what's rightfully yours."

"I appreciate your concern, Ross." She loved him for it. "He must be some kind of lawyer to take on my father-in-law's empire. But when you sent that letter inviting us to the ranch, I know for a fact your good will didn't extend to engaging legal counsel worth thousands of dollars to help out a stranger." Kit wished her voice wouldn't tremble. "You and I both know what it would take."

"For a fallen veteran's wife and child, this attorney would work out a plan that will be feasible and mutually beneficial. All I have to do is give him a call."

"Is there no end to your goodness?" She leaned forward to kiss his cheek. "The truth is, after Winn died I made up my mind that Andy and I would leave with the clothes on our backs, my paltry savings and never look back. I've witnessed the way Charles treats people when they oppose him. I want no part of it."

"Kit—" he whispered with urgency.

The pathos she felt from him was too much to handle. "Have you forgotten what *you* did? You left for the military with the clothes on your back and nothing else. Look at you now! You've made a whole new life for yourself and have become a rancher. Buck left his father's business to do the same thing. You and your partners are making it on hard work and faith despite your chronic health concerns. That's what I intend to do."

His hands formed fists at his side. "But I didn't have a child dependent on me."

"Millions of other people do, and they still make their own way no matter how hard and unfair. When my parents were killed, they'd been living paycheck to paycheck and only left a small insurance policy.

"My grandmother had to take over my support when she was already living in a rented house on a meager fixed income. My grandfather's pension barely covered the necessities. But she did it, and I was given a wonderful life!

"Now it's my turn to do the same thing for Andy, and *I'm* going to do it. After I told Florence I was leaving she said, and I quote, 'You have no skills, no resources. Nothing. How can you possibly care for our grandson?'

"Well, I'm going to show her how. I'm actually quite excited about it. I never want to be beholden to anyone again for my welfare. Thank you for your willingness to find me an attorney, but it isn't needed."

"What they've done to you is morally wrong."

"I know you can't comprehend it because you're such an honorable man, but please don't be outraged for my sake. It's all water under the bridge and has been for years." Putting on her best face, she said, "Andy and I are looking forward to the campout. When do you plan to leave?"

"Midmorning after I've assembled all our gear."

"We'll be packed and ready." She walked him to the door and opened it. There would be no repeat of what had happened earlier when he'd kissed her until she thought she might faint. "Good night, Ross."

ROSS DROVE TO the rear entrance of the ranch house to park, troubled by so many things, but most of all for one statement she'd made. *I never want to be beholden to anyone again for my welfare.*

How far had she thought it through? Did that mean she was ruling out ever getting married again? *Could you blame her, Livingston?*

Once inside, he headed for his bedroom. It was ten-thirty, but he had a vital phone call to make to Sam Donovan in Houston. He disliked bothering anyone this late, but it was an emergency.

After the speech she obviously hadn't planned to make until he'd forced it, Ross felt gutted. Talk about ten years of being in a velvet-lined prison. It pained him what she'd had to live through.

Pleased that he'd reached Sam, Ross didn't waste any time explaining the reason for his call.

"What an astonishing story. I think Charles Wentworth has been off his rocker for a long time. Don't worry about this. I'll do some preliminary groundwork first thing in the morning and see what I come up with. Without looking into the matter of a will and funds due the spouse, here's what I can tell you up front.

"The death gratuity payment is $100,000 for those who died of hostile actions and occurred in a designated combat operation or combat zone or while training for combat or performing hazardous duty. Their lawful surviving spouse is the first in order to receive payment by the CAR assigned to the reporting or assistance base within twenty-four hours of the member's death."

Ross bit down so hard, he almost cracked a tooth. "Kit never saw one dime of that payment. Charles has defrauded her in that area alone."

"She's definitely got a case, even without looking into the existence of a will. If you can talk her into filing a suit, I believe she'll recover a great deal more money. Unfortunately, this is Charles Wentworth we're talking about. He won't play by the rules."

Ross coughed. "I know. My father never did, either."

"That's a fact."

"It's why I'm appealing to you."

"I appreciate that. As soon as I know anything, I'll get back to you. It's an honor for me to do something really important for a retired marine who served our country with distinction. I've always been very proud of you. In my opinion, you're the finest Livingston of them all."

Ross hardly knew what to say. "Those words mean the world to me. Thank you."

"You're welcome. We'll stay in close touch."

With that accomplished, he hung up and took a shower. Anything to help relax him after the horrific revelations Kit had unfolded to him earlier. Otherwise sleep wouldn't come for a while.

Before getting under the covers, he checked his phone messages. One was left by Millie Sands, a forest ranger he'd taken to dinner last month. She wanted to know if he'd like to go to a party with him on Saturday night. He left her a message telling her he had another commitment, but thanked her and told her he'd talk to her soon.

The other message was from his sister Georgianna. She told him to call her back no matter how late, but that it wasn't an emergency. Wondering what it was all about, he phoned her now, knowing he'd be too busy in the morning getting ready for the campout.

"Hey, Georgie Porgie—" He hadn't talked to her in several weeks.

"*Ross*— At last! I've been waiting hours!"

She hadn't phoned more than a half hour ago, but he didn't take issue with his dramatic sister. He hadn't seen her since March when he'd flown home from Walter Reed before coming here. "How's Doug?"

"He's fine. We both are."

"Where is he?"

"Busy flying all over Texas with Scott and Mom and the staff to help Dad on the campaign trail. I'm with them, too, but broke away long enough to phone you. Ross—you've got to come back home. The election's in November. Dad needs you. You promised him that when the summer was over, you'd give up this ranching idea."

Ross coughed and shook his head. "I never promised him."

"But you told him you'd think about it."

"No. That was simply wishful thinking on his part and you know it. He'll never change."

"I know," she admitted.

At twenty-two she'd been crowned Miss Bluebonnet of Texas. That was three years ago. With glistening black hair and blue eyes the color of the famous Texas flower, she was a real beauty like their society mother.

"Did you know Amanda is still waiting for you to come home and marry her?"

"Is *that* what this call is all about?"

"Don't get mad. She's gorgeous and you're already thirty-one. Dad says it's time you were married."

If his sister ever got a look at Kit, then she'd know what gorgeous was.

"Dad was saying that to me eight years ago," he teased. "If I'd been in love with her, I wouldn't have gone into the marines."

"Why *did* you go? Don't you think it's time you leveled with me?"

He closed his eyes. "If I told you the truth, you'd be offended and hurt. I don't want to do that to you."

"It's because Dad's a politician and you aren't. Right?"

"He thrives on that rat race all right, but that's not the reason I went into the military." Ross took a deep breath. "I wonder if you're capable of handling the truth."

"Thank you very much, brother dear."

"I didn't mean that the way it sounded."

"I know you think I'm some empty headed has-been beauty queen who has no substance."

Kit had accused him of thinking the same thing about her. Meeting Kit had given him new insights.

"You know better than that." The hurt in Georgianna's voice decided him to be honest. He confided the secrets of his life to her, leaving little out. When he'd finished, he heard her crying.

"I had no idea, Ross. No idea at all. I love you that much more for being strong enough to be your own person. I just wish you didn't live so far away from Houston. I missed you so terribly when you left home."

She was a sweetie. Always had been.

"I've missed you, too. Those words mean everything to me, Georgie. Naturally I want Dad to be successful, but that life isn't for me."

"I get that now." She sniffed. "Have you ever told our parents what you've told me?"

"No. After I made the decision to leave Harvard, I simply explained that I wanted to serve our country and nothing could persuade me otherwise. They couldn't argue with that because it was for a good cause."

"But you came back with that awful coughing disease. It almost killed all of us."

"Just remember that I'm alive and doing so much better than I was back in March. They know that because I talk to them once a month."

"Ross? Do you mind if I talk to them and try to help them understand?"

"You can if you want, but it won't do any good. I've got big plans for this ranch, honey."

That well had to be a producer! If he hadn't joined up with Carson and Buck, he would never have met Kit. "When they've come to fruition, I'll invite all of you here. Maybe when they see my life, they'll begin to understand."

"I hope so. Before we hang up, just tell me one thing. Is there a special woman in your life yet?"

He'd been honest with his sister about his past. Why not go all the way? "There could be."

"Only could?"

Ross gripped the phone tighter. "It's early days yet." He had his work cut out to convince her they belonged together.

"Can you tell me anything about her? I'll keep it a secret. I just want to know because I love you so much and can't bear for you not to have someone wonderful in your life."

Maybe he'd changed, or maybe she'd just grown more empathetic. Maybe it was a combination of both. Whatever the reason, he felt like confiding in her. "She's a widow with a nine-year-old boy."

A slight gasp escaped. "She has to be one of the mothers you invited to the dude ranch."

"That's right. You'd like her and Andy a lot."

Quiet reigned on her end for a full minute. "Then I'm going to hope it works out. I'd love to meet her."

"Maybe one day I'll bring her and Andy to Houston to meet my family."

"You deserve a great love, Ross. Call me if you ever need to talk. I love you."

"I love you, too. We'll keep in closer touch from now on. I promise."

"I'd like that more than anything. Bye for now."

He rang off and buried his head in the pillow. By the time they got back from the campout, he needed to have convinced Kit not to leave for Texas because there was something much more important waiting for her right here.

She had her heart set on owning a bookstore. He understood that. He also understood that her best friend lived in Galveston. But why not choose a town closer to the ranch where they could see each other, like Jackson or Afton?

Ignited by that idea, he got out of bed and went over to the desk for his laptop. After carrying it back to the bed, he lay down on his stomach and started checking some real estate websites for the sale of commercial businesses. For a half hour he pored over the information and found several possibilities that could be converted. He also noted twelve small bookstores existing in the two towns. Someone might want to sell, or at least hire her.

In the morning he'd go downstairs and print off what he'd found. At the right moment he'd show the results to Kit and ask her to think about it. The possibility that she'd be leaving Jackson for good was insupportable to him.

Ever since she'd mentioned Galveston, it had been in the back of his mind that the beach pad would be the perfect safe house for them in a protected environment. Her son needed normalcy with friends and school and all that went to make up his child's world.

The problem was, she would never accept charity from him, and he wouldn't let her live there without him. His life was here.

The next best thing would be for him to fly down there twice a month and stay at his beach pad so he could see them. A long-distance relationship was the last thing he wanted, but he'd do it if he had to. She was that important to him.

But are you that important to her, Livingston? That was the big question, the one that haunted him until he knew no more.

Chapter Nine

"Everybody ready to roll?" Kit and the children had assembled at the rear of the ranch house with Ross.

"Yes!" the kids cried in unison. Their excitement was contagious.

"Have you got your cameras? Sunscreen? Candy?"

"Yes!"

"Is Fred with us?"

"No!" Johnny blurted before breaking into laughter.

"That's a relief."

Ross grinned at Kit. He'd just packed up the truck with all the camping equipment they'd need. She decided to sit in the truck bed with the children while they drove through the forest, but she couldn't help sneaking glances at his hard-muscled frame as he moved around checking everything. His gaze caught her looking at him several times, causing her pulse to race.

His partners and their wives would drive up to sleep over and bring dinner. For now, Kit and Ross were in charge. She felt the heavy responsibility, but she had Ross with her to share it. He was amazing.

"Remember, guys. There's going to be a summer storm in the early afternoon, but it will pass. If anyone wants to stay home, let me know now."

Kit saw the children look at each other, but no one spoke up.

He walked over to Jenny. "How about you? Are you nervous, honey?"

No one was more caring than Ross. Kit's admiration for him just kept growing.

"A little," she answered honestly, "but I still want to come."

"I get a little scared, too," Kit confided. "We'll sit and watch it together until it's over. How does that sound?"

"Good." Jenny smiled.

"Isn't anyone worried about me? I'm going to get lonely in the cab all by myself."

"Mom—why don't you sit with Ross?"

Warmth crept into her cheeks. Andy had a little imp in him. He was learning it from Johnny. The two of them had been doing more talking. No doubt plotting.

"I promised to sit back here and make sure you children are all right."

"I guess that's that, then!" Ross sent her a look that warned her there'd be a penalty. A curl of excitement ran through her. "So we're off with a Hi-yo, Silver!"

With that comment they all laughed. It sparked a conversation about the Lone Ranger and Hopalong Cassidy.

He drove away from the ranch house and took the road they'd traveled yesterday. There were more clouds in the sky, but it was still a beautiful day. It wasn't hard to pretend they were a family out for an adventure. Kit didn't want any of it to end. For today she'd simply enjoy the delights of being with Ross in this little part of heaven.

Along the way he stopped the truck at an overlook.

Here they got out to take pictures and enjoy a sweeping view of Jackson Hole and the panorama of the spectacular Tetons. With the fast-moving clouds gathering, it took her breath.

They eventually drove on and started climbing through the pines. The higher they drove, the darker it became because of the towering trees and the approaching storm. A change in the weather added a mysterious element to the landscape the children could feel as they gazed about in wonder. She heard thunder rumble in the distance. Before she could say anything, Ross stopped the truck and got out.

"This storm's going to be exciting. Let's get you inside the cab while I throw the tarp over the back." He reached for Jenny. "Down you go, honey." The boys climbed out.

Ross's eyes lifted to hers. "You last," he said as the children scrambled inside the truck. With effortless strength he lifted her out, crushing her against his hard body. Before he let her feet touch the ground he kissed her on the mouth.

"That wasn't fair," she whispered shakily.

"I don't always play fair. You're going to find out all sorts of things about me this trip."

On legs weak as water, she walked to the back door. "Andy? If you'll ride in front with Ross, I'll sit back here between Jenny and Johnny."

"Okay." He sounded happy about it.

In a minute Ross joined them, and they started on their way again. Around another curve and they came out of the trees just as the sky lit up.

"Whoa!" Johnny cried. "That lightning was close."

"It's really far away," Ross said over his shoulder, "but it's so bright it's like daylight."

Kit put her arms around both children. "This is exciting being together like this." More lightning flashes lit their way up the mountain as they wound in and out of the trees. The thunder cracked and shook the ground.

"Pretty spectacular, huh?" He reached over to rub Andy's head. "This makes the Fourth of July fireworks look like a couple of candles on a birthday cake."

His comment made everyone laugh. "We need some heat if we're going to enjoy the show." He turned it on and they kept going. Under normal weather conditions, it wouldn't be dark till nightfall, but the thunderheads were moving in fast, blocking out the light. "We're almost to the meadow. This is better than going to an outdoor movie."

Andy turned to Ross. "I've never been to one. Is it fun?"

"Yup. Especially when I could drive and take a girlfriend."

What would it have been like to be his girlfriend? Kit would never know and needed to put him out of her mind, but the kiss he'd given her was still on her lips, making that impossible.

"I would have loved to take you to one, honey, but we know why I didn't."

"Yeah. I know."

"When my grandmother was alive, she drove us to the drive-in between Providence and Woonsocket. That was one of our favorite things to do. We'd buy treats, and she'd let me sit on the hood of the car with a blanket and pillow to watch the movie."

"I want to do that."

"We will," Ross declared. "One of these days we'll take a balloon ride to Cody and go to the outdoor movie there in a rental car."

Kit wished he wouldn't say things like that to Andy when he knew her plans.

"Can we?" Andy cried.

"Can we go, too?" the other kids asked.

"I don't see why not." When Ross looked at Kit through the rearview mirror, it was like one of those lightning bolts spiking the atmosphere had just gone through her.

Suddenly there was another flash that illuminated the forest. In that instant they caught sight of an enormous elk with an even more enormous rack of antlers crossing the road.

"Ross!" Johnny cried. "Did you see that?"

"It's the same one I took a picture of last month. That's the granddaddy you've been dying to see. He must be nine feet from nose to rump and sure gets around. Wait till you tell your dad you finally saw him."

Johnny bounced up and down on the seat in reaction. Just then another giant thunderclap shook the ground. Andy let out a yelp that caused Ross to laugh. "We're perfectly safe."

Ross brought the truck to the edge of the clearing but still under the dense shelter of the trees. For the next little while they huddled together to watch nature's show. Ross passed out licorice for everyone. When the hail came down the size of marbles, it filled up the windshield and covered the ground. Soon it was followed by a downpour of rain that drowned out every other sound.

"Now you know how people felt who got in the ark with Noah."

"Would *you* have gone in it, Ross?"

"I'd like to think so, Andy."

"Me, too."

"Me, too," Kit echoed with the other children. "Can you believe that at this time yesterday there wasn't a cloud in the sky? The quick changes in weather are a constant source of wonder to me. I can see why you love it here so much. It's like the earth has been baptized. There's no place like it."

Ross turned in the seat so he could look back at her. "Certainly not in Texas."

"Not in Maine either," Andy piped up, sounding very grown up just then.

Both comments disturbed her in more ways than one.

In a few minutes the rain turned to drizzle. "The storm has passed over us. Pretty soon the sun will be peeking out of the clouds again. Keep watching for the elk."

They all kept their eyes peeled. "I can't see him," Johnny complained.

"He's probably sought shelter under a big pine by now where it's dry and he can eat."

"What does he eat?" Andy wanted to know.

Ross let out a cough. "Grass and low-growing plants, about twelve pounds a day."

"Twelve?"

"Yup, and ten gallons of water."

"My daddy says an elk has four stomachs," Jenny informed them.

"Whoa!"

"Can we get out now, Uncle Ross?" Johnny was getting restless. "The rain has stopped."

"You can as soon as I drive out into the clearing. After I remove the tarp, we'll eat sandwiches and go for a hike."

IT HAD BEEN a day to remember. That evening Ross's partners arrived in the Jeep with hot food because they'd dispensed with the idea of building a bonfire. Ross couldn't recall ever having this much fun. Everyone pitched in before going to bed. All food had been put away in the bear locker in Carson's Jeep parked away from them.

While Kit talked with the girls, it was Andy who worked right alongside him like a buddy as they erected the last of the three-man tents.

"Here. Have some more licorice on me."

"Thanks. I wish—" Suddenly he stopped talking.

"What do you wish, Andy?" he prodded.

"Oh, nothing."

"That didn't sound like nothing to me. Tell me what's on your mind."

The boy averted his eyes. "I wish Mom would buy a bookstore in Jackson. Then we wouldn't have to move to Texas."

Ross had to fight his sudden rush of adrenaline. The papers he'd printed out early that morning were burning a hole in his back pocket. "Texas isn't a bad place. I grew up there."

"Yeah, but I don't know anybody there."

"I thought your mom said you were friends with Nila and her daughter."

"I am, kind of, but I really like Johnny and Jenny."

No one could help liking those two children. "I'm sure the idea of moving to a brand-new place makes you feel nervous. But just remember your mom loves you, and she's going to do everything she can to make you happy."

"I know." Andy helped him lay out the three sleeping bags. "Were you nervous when you came out here after the hospital?"

"Very nervous, but in a different way." He coughed.

"How do you mean?"

"I'd already made friends with Carson and Buck, but I was afraid I might not be good at ranching. There was so much to learn."

"You can do everything!"

"You know how to make a guy feel good, but you should have seen me in the beginning. Carson told me it was like he was teaching a kindergartner."

Andy grinned. "He was just teasing."

Kit's boy just kept growing on him. "I guess what I'm trying to say is, what if I didn't like it after I got here and then had to let the guys down because I didn't want to stay? It upset me so much that I might disappoint them, I didn't feel very good for a while."

"But you love it now, right?"

Ross nodded. "More than anything in my whole life. Maybe that's how you'll feel about Galveston after you've been there a while."

Andy didn't respond to that. "Do you miss Texas?"

"Let me put it this way. It's where I was born, and my family lives there, so it will always have a place in my heart. But as I told you before, I wasn't happy there. Do you think you're going to miss Bar Harbor?"

"Not now that my dad's gone."

"I can understand that."

"Mom says she's glad we're moving. I am, too, but I'd rather move here. I like it a lot. Johnny and Jenny told me they love it here more than anything and wouldn't ever want to leave."

This ranch had a stranglehold on all of them.

"Have you told her how you really feel about all this, Andy?"

"I'm afraid to."

"Why? She's not scary." He turned on the Coleman lantern to make sure it worked. "You're her son, right? You always talk everything over, so why don't you tell her what's on your mind? All she can say is no."

"But I don't want her to say no."

He chuckled. "Maybe she'll surprise you. Today she kept saying how much she loved it here."

"I know, but she's already made plans with Nila."

"Plans can be changed. She hasn't bought a bookstore yet or paid money for an apartment." Her money problems made him break out in a cold sweat. Maybe because of talking to Andy like this, Ross would be struck by one of those lightning bolts that had lit up the forest hours earlier, but he didn't care.

"I guess I could talk to her."

"You've got time. You haven't even finished your whole vacation here yet. Maybe tomorrow night or the next when you're back at the cabin. I know she'll listen to you. She loves you to death."

"I love her, too. You're going to sleep in here with us tonight, aren't you?"

Ross had been waiting for that invitation. He coughed. "I was planning on it, provided it's okay with your mom. Otherwise I'll sleep in the back of the truck. Have you ever camped out overnight before?"

"No. Once my dad took me sailing and we stayed out overnight."

"Just the two of you?"

"No. Grandfather came, too, but he got seasick."

"That's one memory I bet you'll never forget."

They were both laughing when they heard, *"Knock, Knock."* Kit lifted the tent flap and came in. "You were both in here so long, I wondered if you'd fallen asleep."

"No," Andy murmured.

Ross smiled. "We were just talking and time got away from us."

"Everybody has gone to bed."

"Then I'll leave the tent while you and Andy get ready."

He stepped outside and looked up at the sky. A few clouds partially hid the moon, shrouding parts of the Grand Teton. One day his house would sit on this spot where their three tents had been pitched. When Ross had been flown home from Kandahar to Walter Reed half dead, he could never have dreamed up a night like this, in a place like this, with a woman like Kit Wentworth.

"Ross?" Andy called to him from the tent door. "Mom says you can come in anytime."

More progress. She hadn't relegated him to the truck. Though she'd done it for Andy's sake, he'd like to think she wanted him inside with them, too. "Thanks. I'll be right there."

After a trip into the forest, he was ready for bed and found Andy in the middle sleeping bag. Kit was over on the other side, leaving him guardian of the tent door.

He removed his Levi jacket and boots, then turned off the lantern and climbed in his bag.

"Good night, you two."

"Good night," she said.

"Thanks for bringing us up here, Ross."

"You're welcome, sport."

Andy turned a couple of times in his bag. Pretty soon Ross could hear the kind of breathing that meant he'd fallen asleep.

Before long he heard sounds of movement coming from the other bag. "Ross?" Kit whispered.

"Yes?"

"Thank for being so good to Andy."

"He's a wonderful boy."

"I can see changes in him. All the worries he's had bottled up are coming out. He's talking more than he has in years. It's because of you."

"I can't take the credit. When you told him he didn't have to live with his grandparents anymore, you're the one who changed history for him."

"But you have to know you're the one representing security right now. Andy lost what little he had when his father died."

"You're not giving yourself any credit. You're his mother. Don't you know you're his whole world?"

"He's my whole world, too," Kit said quietly. "But

until that letter from the ranch came, I didn't know where to turn. I'm afraid you've become his hero."

"Why afraid? I've never been anyone's hero and kind of like the idea."

"Joke all you want, but it's true. In fact, it has me worried."

He sat up. "For what reason?"

"Last night he told me that now Winn was gone, he wished you could be his dad." The words sank deep in Ross's soul, causing his heart rate to triple. "Apparently he and the other children have been doing a lot of talking about the recent changes in their lives. I'm afraid Andy's going to talk to you about it, and I want you to be prepared."

Ross needed to maneuver his way carefully through this minefield. "Do you know when I was in the hospital, I got pretty down and worried I might never have a family of my own. Since you came, I've been thinking how great it would be to have a son like Andy."

"But if you were to tell him that to make him happy, he'd hang on to it."

"I'd only tell him that because it's true. Would that be such a bad thing?"

"You know it would."

"Because you'll be in Texas."

"Yes."

"Wherever you go there's nothing wrong with Andy knowing he's got a friend who loves him here in the Tetons. Yesterday when you were talking to the sheriff, that son of yours climbed right into my heart. You couldn't see what I saw. Andy stood next to you without flinching. For a moment I felt like I was back in Afghanistan.

"We occasionally came across a broken-down car in the road with a mother asking for help, her son at her side willing to protect her, a fearless expression on his face. I never knew if they were the enemy lying in wait. I always held my breath as I approached, anticipating fireworks.

"Andy dealt with the fireworks like a man. The truth is, I couldn't love that boy more if he were my own son. Considering he and I were raised the same way in terms of the emotional and financial environment, plus the domination factor, it's not so strange that we've bonded this fast."

"You're right," she admitted in a croaky voice.

"His vulnerability makes him that much more lovable. I don't need to tell you how terrific he is. Don't worry that he might talk to me about his feelings. He already has."

"What has he said?" She sounded alarmed.

"He's told me he doesn't want to live in Texas. He likes Nila and her daughter well enough, but he really likes Johnny and Jenny and wishes you would buy a bookstore in Jackson so you can live there. I told him that, given time, he might learn to love Texas the way I love the ranch. That's the way we left our conversation. The point is, we're buddies whatever happens in the future. I'll always be his friend."

Silence filled the interior of the tent.

He lay back down. Having delivered his salvos, he hoped they kept her tossing and turning until morning.

For the first time since she'd come to the ranch, he knew he was going to get a good night's sleep for a change.

KIT GOT DOWN with Jenny to examine the bluebells that grew in profusion around the end of the lake. "Aren't they beautiful?"

"I want to pick some, but daddy told me I couldn't."

"I know. The problem is, they're wildflowers and they'll die too fast to enjoy them."

She could hear Johnny talking to Ross in the background. "Are you sure there are fish in here?"

"I know there are, but they're not feeding today. Maybe the storm yesterday has caused them to feed on the bottom of the lake. We'll have lots of chances in the future to hike up here again."

"I won't," Andy muttered.

"'Cos you have to go to Texas, huh."

"Yes."

"Hey, guys—I'm afraid it's time for us to hike down to the truck and drive back to the ranch. You have Back To School Night and I promised your folks I'd bring you home in time for baths and dinner first."

"I don't want school to start. I want to stay up here."

Ross chuckled. "When you see all the cute girls in your class, Johnny, you'll change your mind."

"Girls?"

"Yeah. That's why I didn't like my boarding school. There weren't any."

Kit smiled in spite of the dejection she'd heard in Andy's voice seconds ago.

"I like school," Jenny piped up.

Kit put an arm around her. "I liked it, too. That's because you're a reader like me."

"Okay, everybody. Hand me your rods and we'll get going."

They followed Ross down the mountain. Since the conversation with him in the tent last night when he'd left Kit speechless with his admissions, they hadn't discussed anything. He'd been up before she'd awakened. After breakfast the parents had helped them pack everything before they'd left and Ross had led her and the children up to the lake.

The kids did all the conversing, for which she was grateful. She'd lain awake most of the night with a heavy heart. Kit realized she'd sprung the idea of moving to Texas on Andy without any preparation. It was a lot to ask of him, but these were desperate circumstances.

Naturally he'd rather stay in Jackson near people who'd shown him the time of his life. For Andy to want her to buy a business here and live probably shouldn't have surprised her. But after her talks with Nila, she'd been so focused on Texas, it never occurred to her that Andy would even think about her earning her living somewhere else.

Kit was grateful to Ross for being on her side and not trying to influence Andy. He continued to handle her son in a way that left her awed by his depth of understanding.

Her thoughts drifted back to the day she'd received the letter from Carson. She'd thought it had been a mistake, and she'd called Colonel Hodges. But he'd convinced her it was no mistake. Whether she had money or not wasn't the point. These men needed healing, too.

After listening to Ross last night, she understood what the Colonel had meant. Caring for these children who'd lost their fathers had brought fulfillment to the lives of these retired marines. She saw what it had done for three men who'd been discharged for health reasons and had come home low in body and spirit. What they'd done and were doing was a marvel.

As she watched Ross helping the children down the mountain, a feeling of intense love for him swept through her. Though it was too soon, there was no doubt in her mind she'd fallen terribly in love with him.

Terribly, because as much as she wanted to acknowledge her love to him, it meant handing over a part of herself. It meant being at the mercy of a man again. She didn't know if she could ever do that.

When they reached the truck, Kit got in back with the kids, but this time Andy quietly climbed in front with Ross. She understood. The sand was emptying from the top of the hourglass. The few days left to be with him were precious.

Later, after they'd dropped Johnny off at his house, they pulled into the parking area outside the ranch house. Andy came around as Kit and Jenny got down from the tailgate. She waved goodbye and ran around the corner to find her nana.

"Mom? After dinner Ross is going to take us for a horseback ride down by the river while the kids go over to school with their parents."

Her body quivered at the mere thought. "That's really nice of him, but aren't you tired after all the hiking we've done?"

"Heck, no. He says the horses need the exercise."

"Let's hurry to the cabin then and take a shower first."

"Why? We'll just get grubby again."

Kit couldn't fault his logic. "Maybe the horses would like it if we smelled better."

"Mom!" He ran over to tell Ross what she'd said.

Deep rich laughter poured out of him. Their eyes met for a moment in pure amusement before a look crept into his that made her legs tremble. "Let's freshen up inside and eat."

She nodded and hurried around to the entrance with Andy. It hadn't taken but one hour of arriving at the ranch on Saturday with Ross to get into the habit of eating, sleeping and having the time of their lives in between. But the fun was going to stop. The more she thought about it, the more she couldn't bear it.

Darkness had settled over the ranch by the time Ross drove them back to their cabin from the stable. After he pulled to a stop, he turned to them. "I'm going to give you an hour, then I'm coming by to drive you to my home where you'll stay with me until you leave the ranch."

Andy's eyes rounded. "But Buck hasn't built it yet!"

"That's true. I'm talking about the home I live in right now. The whole upstairs of the ranch house is mine. I have my own apartment. The other one across the hall used to be the one for Buck. Since I've lived in Wyoming, I've never invited anyone upstairs before. You'll be the first ones."

"Can we, Mom?"

He captured her gaze. "After sleeping with you in

the tent last night, the thought of sleeping alone doesn't sound like much fun."

She knew what he was really telling her. He'd had his share of women, but no woman had passed over his threshold while he'd been living here. But he also had another more compelling agenda. For some reason he wanted her and Andy under the ranch house roof from here on out.

This had to do with Charles, otherwise Ross wouldn't be making such an unprecedented decision. As usual, he was handling it in a way that wouldn't alarm Andy.

Kit knew what she ought to reply to protect her heart, but her son's shining eyes defeated her. "Well, since we'll be your first guests, we can hardly turn down your gracious invitation. Maybe we should find a tree outside in the morning and carve your initials. 'AW slept here.'"

"Make it AW and K and we'll do it," Ross murmured.

"Cool!"

"Why don't you hurry and shower first, honey."

"You can wear your pajamas over, sport."

"Okay." After he'd gone inside the cabin she turned to Ross. "What's happened?"

"Your father-in-law left a message at the front desk. You're to expect a visitor sometime between now and tomorrow morning. I know you can handle him, but I'd rather you had some warning than simply answering your cabin door to him."

"So would I. Thank you, Ross."

He nodded. "I'll be back."

Kit hurried inside. Andy had already gotten in the shower. She started packing as fast as she could. They hadn't brought much with them, so it was no huge chore.

Andy came out again in his camouflage pajamas so she could shower.

As she hurried in the bathroom, he said, "I just love him, Mom."

I know you do. So do I.

When they were ready, Kit did a once-over of the cabin to make sure they hadn't left anything before she went outside to the truck. Ross helped her inside next to Andy, and they took off.

He parked at the rear of the ranch house. Together they carried their things down a hallway that led to the staircase.

"This is fun. I've never seen this part of the ranch house before."

"It's about time you did," he said on a cough.

Buck was just coming out of the office and saw them. His eyes widened. "Hey—what's going on?"

"Ross is moving us into your old apartment!"

A half smile broke out on his face. "Is that right?"

"Yeah. He says he's been lonely."

"That's a fact. Jenny and Alex are going to be thrilled to have friends around this place."

Kit smiled. "We're happy about it, too, believe me."

Buck's gaze drifted to Ross. "What can I do to help?"

"Thanks, but Andy and I have it covered. How did Back To School Night go?"

"Pretty well, but they've put the kids in two separate classes. That kind of upset them. Alex is going to go over there in the morning and see what she can do to keep them together. We're hoping that when the administration understands the uniqueness of their situation, they'll cooperate."

"I'm sure they will," Kit said to assure him.

"See you guys in the morning."

As Buck waved them off, the three of them went up the stairs. Ross opened the door to the empty apartment and set down the suitcases. "This has a living/dining area and kitchenette, a bedroom with a queen and a twin bed, a bathroom and a small study. Housekeeping made this place ready for occupancy after Buck moved downstairs, so you should be perfectly comfortable."

"Hey, Mom." Andy put down the case he was holding and ran through the apartment to the study. "This is great!" He came hurrying back. "Where's your apartment?"

"Right across the hall. It looks exactly like yours. While we were building the cabins, Buck did some remodeling up here in the spring to update everything."

"It's lovely," Kit murmured, looking around. She lowered her case to the carpeted floor. "How lucky can Andy and I be?"

He flashed them a smile. "I'm glad you like it."

"Thanks for letting us stay up here."

"You're welcome." Ross couldn't resist giving Andy a hug. "Now it's cozy."

"I always felt lonely at my grandfather's. My bedroom was on another floor from my mom's, and he wouldn't let me keep a light on."

"Oh, honey." Kit threw her arms around her son. "I felt lonely, too, more than you'll ever know."

"But those days are over, right?" Ross high-fived him.

"Right."

He glanced at Kit. "Let's program each other's phone numbers right now."

"Good idea."

Once that was done, he said, "I know you're tired, so I'll say good-night. Sleep well."

"Thanks to you, we will."

After he left, Kit put on her pajamas and opened the case with their toiletries so Andy could brush his teeth. "Could I sleep with you tonight?"

"You mean in the big bed?"

"Yes."

"I'd love it." Unlike other children, he had never been allowed to creep in their bedroom. For the first year after her parents had died, many was the night Kit had slept with her grandmother. "Come on. We'll read the second chapter of *Call of the Wild*."

After he said his prayers and dived under the covers, she opened another suitcase to retrieve the book. The lamp at the bedside table shed enough light for her to read. A few pages into it, he said in a sleepy voice, "Judge Miller was kind to Buck...just like Ross is to me." A lone tear trickled out of his eye before he fell sound asleep.

Moved beyond words, she got out of bed. After putting on her terry cloth robe, she tiptoed out of the bedroom and shut the door. Without conscious thought she opened the door to the apartment and slipped across the hall. She could see light under his door and heard coughing before she knocked. In a second it opened to reveal the dark-haired cowboy who'd walked into her life last week and refused to go away.

In the semidark he stood there wearing only the bottom half of a pair of navy sweats. The dusting of black hair on his well-defined chest added to his male potency. She tried to smother the quiet gasp that escaped at the sight of him.

Lost for words she studied the cleft in his chin. Gazing at the lines of his hard mouth and handsome features, she couldn't quite catch her breath.

"Forgive me. I shouldn't have bothered you this late, but when I was reading to Andy just now, he said something before he fell asleep I felt you should hear."

"Come in," he urged.

"I can't. He might wake up and wonder where I am. I was reading to him from Jack London's book. As his eyes fluttered closed, he said something so sweet and dear, I wanted you to know. You'll appreciate it because you read that book, too."

When she told him, Ross lifted his right hand and traced her features with his fingers. At his touch, little trickles of delight flowed through her body. "He's an easy boy to love."

"He's never known real kindness like yours, the kind that transforms lives. If it weren't for you, he wouldn't understand how great it is to be a good man, to *want* to be a good man like you. He's in awe of you, Ross. So am I. That's what I came to say."

"Kit..."

Suddenly she was in his arms. His head descended until his mouth covered hers.

She moaned for the sheer ecstasy his hands and lips created. Never in her life had she known hunger like this. At nineteen she'd been in love with love and flattered by Winn's attention, but it hadn't felt anything like this. Not even close.

Ross crushed her against him until there was no space between them. The fire he was whipping up inside her was so hot and intense, she was losing control.

Kit had started this by knocking on his apartment door. Now she had to be the one to end it *before she couldn't.* She slid her hands up his chest to ease herself away, but his reaction was to deepen their kiss. Much as she wanted to go on enjoying this mindless ecstasy, she didn't dare. Somehow she found the strength to tear her mouth from his and pull away.

"Don't leave me," he begged. "I'm in love for the first time in my life. There's no mistaking it for anything else. I want you, Kit. You have no idea how much." His dark brown eyes were glazed over.

"Forgive me for starting this tonight."

He ran his hands up and down her arms. "It's because you want me just as badly."

"You're right." Her voice shook. "But this isn't the time or the place, not when there's so much at stake. I'm afraid to get involved again."

"I understand that, so we'll take this slowly."

"No. That's unfair to you because I can't make any promises. I just can't!" she cried from her soul before wrenching herself from his grasp.

Kit heard him call her name, but she'd already shut and locked her apartment door. Unfortunately it wouldn't keep her in. She would have to exercise the greatest self-control of her life to go to bed and stay there.

While she stood there clutching the back of one of the chairs, her cell phone rang. She reached for it. "Ross?"

"Willy just phoned me. Charles is downstairs in the foyer demanding to talk to you. What would you like to do?"

She took a deep breath. "I'm going to have to talk to him, but we need to be private."

"I'll go down and bring him to your room. Is Andy still asleep?"

"Yes. The door's shut to the bedroom."

"Then there shouldn't be a problem if Charles doesn't raise his voice. Are you ready?"

A calm had settled over her. This confrontation had been coming on for years. "More than ready."

"Good girl."

After she hung up, she walked across the apartment and turned on the overhead light. Then she opened the front door and waited in the hall for him. She heard a cough.

Pretty soon she saw two figures coming toward her. Charles was almost as tall as Ross. But where the black-haired retired marine was hard and lean dressed in a sport shirt and jeans, her father-in-law with his thinning ash-colored hair looked soft and overfed in his suit, despite Florence's regimen.

The only surprise was the suffering she saw on his face when the light fell across him. His gray eyes stared at her for the longest time. "Where's Andrew?"

"Asleep in the bedroom."

Ross eyed her over the older man's shoulder. "I'll be across the hall."

"Call off your bodyguard, Kit. You don't need him."

"If you haven't understood by now, Charles, let me explain I have no use for another man in my life. After living with you and Winn, I don't need any man. Come in and say what you have to say. I'm exhausted and want to go to bed."

Chapter Ten

Ross stared at the closed door.

I don't need any man. I have no use for another man.

Was that said for her father-in-law's sake? Or had she just sent Ross a message? If so, it had chilled his blood because it had sounded so final. Irrevocable.

His mind replayed what had gone on in here before Charles had arrived. When he'd told Kit he was in love for the first time in his life, she'd said nothing back. Though she'd admitted she wanted him, she couldn't make any promises.

Fragmented, he went back inside his apartment, but he left the door ajar so he'd be aware when the other man left. In an agony of thought, he went into his kitchen and made himself a cup of coffee. After draining it, he heard a sound coming from the corridor. When he reached his door, Ross saw the back of Charles as he stormed down the hall toward the stairs.

His first impulse was to rush over there, but her words had left their sting. While he waited for her to come to him, he phoned the front desk. Willy told him Mr. Wentworth just left in a car with another man. Willy had locked the front door behind him.

Ross thanked him and hung up. In another hour of waiting she still hadn't come. There was no phone call.

She's afraid of involvement, Livingston.

He couldn't blame her for that. Not after ten years of being trapped by two men.

Ross got it.

The papers he'd printed off to give her stared up at him from the coffee table. No way would he be giving them to her now. She'd see them as another man attempting to run her life, telling her what she ought to do, as if she didn't have the brains to figure out life for herself.

Before he did anything else, he left a message for Sam Donovan. "Mrs. Wentworth won't be filing a suit. Stop all work on her case and send me the bill." She'd told Ross she didn't want to sue for the money, but he hadn't listened to her. He'd gone ahead and phoned Sam.

Two more days to get through before she left for Texas. What a hell of a time for the kids to be back in school!

If it was all right with Kit tomorrow, he'd take Andy with him to repair some fencing and do a few chores. Let him see what it was like doing regular work on the ranch. They'd pack a lunch. Kit could take a well-earned rest and enjoy the day by herself or with Alex or Tracy.

On Friday they could do a float trip or take a balloon ride. Whatever sounded fun to Andy. Beyond that he wouldn't allow himself to think.

He got ready for bed once more. There was too much silence and too many hours left to try to kill it without help. TV had its uses.

WHEN HE WENT down to breakfast early the next morning, there were still a few empty tables. He spotted Kit immediately. She was wearing a new blouse with jeans he hadn't seen before. Andy sat with her and Jenny while they ate. Everything seemed so normal with Kit, last night's nocturnal activities with Charles Wentworth might never have happened.

If it killed him, Ross would pretend normalcy, too. He gazed at them. "Good morning."

Andy smiled at him. "Hey, Ross."

"How did you sleep?"

"Great!"

Ross had no idea if Andy knew his grandfather had come to the ranch house last night or not.

"Hi, Uncle Ross."

He sat down between the two kids. The waitress came over and poured him a cup of coffee, but he didn't order. The thought of food made him nauseous. "I like your new outfit for school. Are you excited?"

She nodded. "Nana's taking me and Johnny. Andy and Kit are going to drive into Jackson with us."

That took care of part of the morning.

He drank some of the steaming liquid to fill the growing pit in his stomach before he flicked a glance to Kit. She was just finishing the last of her omelet. "When you get back, I'll be at the south pasture. Give me a ring, and I'll take you on an afternoon float trip."

"Could we, Mom?"

"I'd love it."

"Then I'll see all of you later."

"See ya," Andy responded.

He couldn't deal with this any longer and got to his

feet. On his way out of the dining room he ran into Alex in the foyer. "Big day for Jenny."

"For me, too. I brought the van around to the front. Oh, Ross, I want her to like her new school."

"Of course she will. I understand Kit and Andy are driving in with you."

"Yes. I'm going to do a little shopping, and she said she'd like to do some, too."

"Have fun then and stop worrying. We all got through our first day of school, right?"

She laughed. "I needed to hear you say that. Tell that to Buck. He's more of a nervous wreck than I am."

Alex didn't know the half of it. Seeing black, Ross bolted off down the back hallway for the rear door.

Eight hours later Ross was in the office on the phone with Mac Dawson when another call came in. His adrenaline surged when he saw who it was. After getting off fast with the oil man, he clicked on.

"Kit?" It was late. Tracy had already brought the kids home from school over an hour ago.

"Hi. Sorry that the day got away from us and ruined the plans for that float trip. I hope it didn't put you out too much."

How about my shattered dreams? "Not at all."

"Would it be possible for you to pick up me and Andy in town? If not, we can take a taxi back to the ranch."

He let out the breath he'd been holding. "Where are you?"

"At Pinky G's Pizzeria on Broadway Street having an early dinner."

Somehow he had to go on playing the cordial host

until he drove her to the airport on Saturday morning. "I'll be there within a half hour."

"Thank you. We'll be outside watching for you."

Totally gutted, he strode swiftly out of the ranch house and started up the truck. He accelerated faster than he should have, passing other cars to reach the highway. When he drove into town, he spotted them in front of the restaurant. She was so attractive it took him a second to realize she wasn't holding any packages. That surprised him.

Ross slowed down and leaned across the seat to open the door for them. "Hey—" He smiled at Andy who slid in first. After Kit had shut the door he took off, heading for the main artery leading out of town. "Did you have a good day?"

"Yeah. Thanks for picking us up."

"I was glad to. What did you do?"

"All kinds of stuff." Which told him nothing.

"After the kids got home from school, they wondered where you were."

"How was their first day?" Kit asked.

"I couldn't tell. They're swimming right now."

"That's what I want to do." Andy looked at him. "What did you do today?"

"I had a meeting with my partners, and we made the decision to start the drilling for the well on Monday."

"That's wonderful news," she exclaimed.

Right now he couldn't appreciate it. Before long they were back at the ranch. Ross was coughing more than usual and needed his inhaler. He got out and walked upstairs with them.

"That doesn't sound good," Kit said in alarm.

"I'll be all right." Sometimes sleep deprivation made his condition worse. Last night was the worst he'd ever lived through since coming to the ranch.

Andy looked anxious, too. "Are you sure?"

"I just need my medicine. If you'll excuse me, I'll see you two downstairs later for a game of Ping-Pong."

"I'm not very good at it."

"Neither am I, but we'll still have fun."

"Yeah."

Ross entered his apartment and shut the door. Once he'd used his inhaler, he intended to lie down. Sleep was what he needed to find forgetfulness. But before the medicine kicked in, he heard a knock on the door.

"Andy?"

"No. It's Kit. He's gone down to the pool. May I come in, or is it a bad time?"

Those were the words he'd been waiting for last night after Charles had left, but they'd never come. He walked through the apartment and unlocked the door, still coughing. "Are you sure you want to?"

"Yes," she said with enough emotion that he knew she meant it.

He opened the door wider so she could enter. "You're not well."

"It'll pass in a minute."

"Does it help to lie down?"

"Not really, but I often do because the medication makes me sleepy."

"Then, please, do it."

"What's so important?"

"Our lives." Her voice shook. She followed him into the bedroom and sat down on a chair while he lay back against some pillows. "Last night Charles came with terms of surrender. He can't bear to lose Andy. There's a house near the mansion he'll buy for me. He'll give me an allowance and won't force Andy to attend that school."

Ross jackknifed into a sitting position. He didn't know Genghis had it in him. His thoughts reeled. "What did you tell him?"

"That he was ten years too late, that Andy and I had other plans. I told him that after Andy and I were settled, he and the family could visit us when they wanted. He got angry and left.

"Andy had been listening from his bedroom the whole time. He came out and we had a talk that lasted a long time. My son told me a lot of things. Above all, Andy has grown to love you and can't understand why I can't live in Jackson and work so we can all be friends.

"He loves it here. I believe it because I love it here, too. Neither of us has ever been to Galveston. It has no appeal for either of us except it's Nila's home and she was willing to help me relocate."

By this time Ross had gotten to his feet. "Does Nila know any of this?"

"Not yet, but she knows what a huge decision we have to make. As I told Andy, she's a mom as well and wants us to be happy. And so do I," she said as a tear slipped down her cheek.

"This morning I told Alex we had several things to do in town and wanted to be dropped off at the Teton Book Shop. I looked it up in the directory thinking I could find out if there was a job opening for a salesperson. I told Alex I'd call you to come and get us so she wouldn't wait."

Ross couldn't believe what he was hearing.

"After leaving the shop, I contacted a Realtor who showed us quite a few rental properties, and we discussed some business opportunities."

"And?" The medicine had started working, but her news had created a new breathing problem for him.

"We've seen one rental house we really like, and the manager at Carter's department store told me they were thinking of making their books area more reader friendly. He liked my ideas for the coffee bar and told me to come back next week and we'd talk about it."

Ross was afraid to trust what he was hearing. "What's really turned things around for you? Aren't you terrified I'll influence Andy and create another crisis for you? Last night I heard you tell Charles you don't need any man."

"I don't, but you're not any man." She moved closer. "You're my guardian angel. I love you so much that the thought of losing the love you say you have for me right now fills me with unbearable anguish." She lifted her eyes to him. "You're everything a woman could desire in a man. I don't even know where to start telling you all the things you mean to me. It scares me I won't be able to live up to you."

His hands cradled her face. "You want to know scared? I'm still learning how to be a rancher like Carson. I don't have a lot to offer yet, but it's the life I love. After I left you and Andy in the cabin that first afternoon, I knew you were the woman I wanted. I knew it in the way you know the sun's going to go down behind the Grand Teton every evening.

"You're the most beautiful woman inside and out I ever met. You talk about *me* being some kind of angel… when I saw the courage you had to run away from a horrific situation in order to free your son, when I felt and witnessed your great love for him, that was it. I had to have you for my own and hoped that one day you could love me half as much as you love him."

She threw her arms around his neck. "Oh, darling—" Kit kissed every inch of his striking features. "I'm so in love with you it hurts."

"Enough to marry me?"

"If you're sure. I come with so much baggage and don't want to be a disappointment to you."

"Oh, Kit—how can I explain what you mean to me? There aren't enough words."

"I feel the same way."

The tight bands squeezing his lungs relaxed, and he began kissing her in earnest. He needed this. She was life to him. He picked her up and carried her over to the bed. Following her down, they began to communicate what they'd been forced to hold back. Instead of being in a frenzy of need, Ross kissed her slowly, deliberately.

"Oh, sweetheart—" He sighed later against her neck as his lips roved over her scented skin. "I've been single for so long, waiting and wondering if I'd ever find fulfillment like my buddies. To be holding the woman of my dreams in my arms at last and know you're mine forever—" Instead of more words, he finished saying them with his mouth.

"This is heaven," she whispered much later. "With

the right man I knew it could be found on earth. But I had to come to the ranch to discover my soul mate. On the campout, Andy wanted to know if I would marry you if you asked me."

"What did you answer him?"

"That you and I barely knew each other, but that didn't stop him. According to Johnny, Carson got married within five weeks. As for Buck, it only took ten days."

Deep, free-floating laughter rumbled out of Ross. "I want to marry you today, this very instant. I'm sure Buck told Alex the same thing. Unlike Tracy, she didn't have a big family to invite."

"But *you* have one, darling. If we wait six weeks, it will give you time to put in that well while I get settled in a job. Then we'll invite both our dysfunctional families out here for our wedding. Maybe they'll see we're truly happy and wish us well, if only for Andy's sake. What do you think?"

"I'd rather invite them for a visit next year when we've built a house and some of my plans to make the ranch operate in the black for a change come to fruition. But all of it can be negotiated because we're equal partners, Kit. I want you to know that."

"I do. I trust you with my life."

"Enough to live upstairs with me until our house is built? I don't want you to move to a rental."

"I don't want to either. I'll pay rent here."

Ross knew not to fight her. He'd learned his lesson. "Fine. Now let's stop talking. Right now there's only one thing I want to do."

He crushed her mouth quiet as desire took over, blotting out the world.

Suddenly they heard Andy's voice calling from the hallway. "Mom?"

Ross moved off her fast and got to his feet so she could sit up, but she was much slower to respond. "Come on in, sport."

When Andy walked in the bedroom, his eyes lit up.

"Hi, honey. I thought you were going to swim."

"We *did* until Buck closed the pool and sent me up here."

They'd been up here a long time. When she darted Ross a guilty look, he just laughed.

"I need to freshen up."

He grabbed her around the waist so she couldn't get away. "Before we go anywhere or do anything, there's something your mom and I want to tell you."

"I already know."

"What do you think you know?" Kit exclaimed.

"Johnny said the reason you and Ross never came down was because you're going to get married."

Both Ross and Kit roared with laughter. "One thing you're going to learn, sweetheart. That kid is psychic, and there are no secrets in this house." Then he sobered and put his hands on his shoulders. He stared at Andy. "I love you, son. It would be an honor to be your new dad."

"I love you so much," he cried and grabbed Ross around the waist.

Ross was moved almost without words. "If it's all right with you, we're thinking about getting married in about six weeks. Maybe by then your grandfather won't be so upset, and he and your grandmother will come." If Kit could forgive them, Ross certainly could.

No words came out of Andy. Only hugs and tears of pure joy.

KIT AND ANDY had just entered the dining room for breakfast the next morning when everyone yelled, "Surprise!"

Ross's partners and their families had assembled at one of the big tables. There were waffles and French toast and bacon and eggs. A real feast. The kids had made a banner fastened to the log wall that said, "Congratulations Kit and Ross," done in their own printing. No doubt Andy's work was in there somewhere.

Her throat swelled with emotion until she couldn't swallow. Ross squeezed her hip. "What a homecoming," he whispered.

The ranch *did* feel like home.

She wiped her eyes and sat down by Johnny. "I can't begin to tell you how much this means to us. Not just because of today, but because of every day since we first arrived. I'm overwhelmed with all the things you've done for us."

"We've enjoyed you, too," Carson murmured.

She stared at the three men. "You know the saying about if you want something done, ask a marine? It has taken on a whole new meaning for me since your letter came inviting us to the ranch. Just know we think the world of all of you and will be forever grateful."

"We're glad you're going to marry Ross." This from Johnny.

He always made her smile. "I feel the same and love

that banner you made for us. It's fantastic! But aren't you guys supposed to be at school?"

"Yup. But we didn't want to go today because daddy said this is a red-letter day, and he made an e-excep-shun."

"Nana says we're going to celebrate." Jenny looked at Andy. "Do you want to go to Funorama?"

"What's that?"

"This real fun place with rides and stuff, and you get to eat pizza."

"Sure! That sounds cool."

Kit smiled at Jenny. "Do you like school, Jenny?"

"I love it."

"How about you, Johnny?"

"It's pretty fun."

"What's your favorite subject?"

"Recess."

More laughter broke out while everyone ate. Toward the end of the meal, Buck tapped his water glass with a fork. "It appears our experiment to honor our fallen soldiers has been a huge success, so we're planning to invite more widows and their children next summer. You children are going to be a big part of it, and we're always going to need your help."

He winked at Ross. "There's only one problem. We don't have any more single men to marry off."

"Yes, we do," Johnny interjected. "Willy!"

Chapter Eleven

Six Weeks Later

Ross was still in the shower. Kit waited feverishly for him to come to bed. When she saw his tall physique in the semidarkness of the master bedroom, it was a surreal moment with the silhouette of the Grand Teton framing him. She reached for her new husband, hungry to belong to him forever.

"My love," he said, his voice thick with emotion. "I didn't think our wedding night would ever come."

"I know. I love you," she cried as they began giving and receiving pleasure she hadn't thought possible. They clung to each other throughout the night, living to make each other happy.

Kit was shocked how late it was when she awakened the next morning tangled up with him, their bed covers askew. She couldn't describe this kind of fulfillment. You had to experience it.

You had to be married to Ross.

She lifted her hand where a gold wedding band with a diamond dazzled her eyes. Mrs. Ross Livingston. What joy!

All of a sudden he coughed. He did it in his sleep.

It wounded her every time. She doubted she'd ever get used to it. Ross teased her, it was his badge of courage, but it was a lot more than that. It was an honor to be married to him. She knew that, and she was determined to be the best wife on earth.

She felt him stir, then he was kissing her again. "Good morning, sweetheart." He pulled her on top of him. "This is what life is all about."

She was too breathless to answer him.

An hour later he opened his eyes and stared into hers. He played with her hair. "Tell me what you're thinking."

"That the ranch house made a beautiful place for a wedding and I could lie here with you forever."

She was aware of time passing. They only had time for a two-day honeymoon. Kit had to be back to work at the department store on Monday. But in reality, since she'd first met Ross, she felt as if she'd been on a continual honeymoon.

Carson and Tracy had insisted the newlyweds stay at their house, and they'd moved in the upstairs of the ranch house for the weekend. Andy was sleeping with Johnny in Buck's old apartment. The guys had arranged for all the cabins to be available this weekend for the wedding guests that included Nila and her family.

"I loved your family, Ross, especially Georgianna."

"I knew you two would get along."

"The look of pride on your father's face when you told him the well was a big producer was priceless."

Ross grinned. "It was, wasn't it? But the big shock was seeing your in-laws show up at the last minute."

"That was a shock all right." Kit and Ross had sent out invitations, but she'd never received an answer from her in-laws and hadn't expected one. "The fact that they came proves to me no one is all bad. They came for Andy, and I know it made him happy."

"I'm sure it did. They should have come, not only to honor their son's boy, but the fabulous mother who raised him. This was the way to do it."

"Yes. I have to tell you I'm so glad I didn't have to sell the ring. One day I'll give it to Andy so he can give it to the woman he loves."

"It'll have great meaning knowing his father gave it to you. I've been waiting until now to give you something else. It's an envelope Charles handed Willy to give to you."

"Did you open it?"

"No, darling. It's for you. I'll get it." He slid out of bed and put on a robe. In a minute he came back in the bedroom with it and handed it to her.

She opened the envelope with her father-in-law's letterhead. Inside she saw a check made out to her for $2,000,000. He'd put in a note. *Winn would have wanted you and Andy to have this. C.*

It was hard to swallow. "My grandmother used to say, faith precedes the miracle."

He covered her face with kisses. "You've taught me that. Faith brought you here. I don't know what I ever did to deserve you, but I'm going to hold on to you for dear life. You and Andy *are* my life now, Kit."

She threw her arms around his neck. "You're *my* miracle. I'll love you till the day I die and beyond."

* * * * *

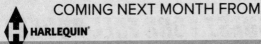

REQUEST YOUR FREE BOOKS!
2 FREE NOVELS PLUS 2 FREE GIFTS!

HARLEQUIN®

American ★ Romance®

LOVE, HOME & HAPPINESS

YES! Please send me 2 FREE Harlequin® American Romance® novels and my 2 FREE gifts (gifts are worth about $10). After receiving them, if I don't wish to receive any more books, I can return the shipping statement marked "cancel." If I don't cancel, I will receive 4 brand-new novels every month and be billed just $4.74 per book in the U.S. or $5.24 per book in Canada. That's a savings of at least 14% off the cover price! It's quite a bargain! Shipping and handling is just 50¢ per book in the U.S. and 75¢ per book in Canada.* I understand that accepting the 2 free books and gifts places me under no obligation to buy anything. I can always return a shipment and cancel at any time. Even if I never buy another book, the two free books and gifts are mine to keep forever.

154/354 HDN F4YN

Name _____ (PLEASE PRINT) _____

Address _____ Apt. # _____

City _____ State/Prov. _____ Zip/Postal Code _____

Signature (if under 18, a parent or guardian must sign) _____

Mail to the **Harlequin® Reader Service:**
IN U.S.A.: P.O. Box 1867, Buffalo, NY 14240-1867
IN CANADA: P.O. Box 609, Fort Erie, Ontario L2A 5X3

Want to try two free books from another line?
Call 1-800-873-8635 or visit www.ReaderService.com.

* Terms and prices subject to change without notice. Prices do not include applicable taxes. Sales tax applicable in N.Y. Canadian residents will be charged applicable taxes. Offer not valid in Quebec. This offer is limited to one order per household. Not valid for current subscribers to Harlequin American Romance books. All orders subject to credit approval. Credit or debit balances in a customer's account(s) may be offset by any other outstanding balance owed by or to the customer. Please allow 4 to 6 weeks for delivery. Offer available while quantities last.

Your Privacy—The Harlequin® Reader Service is committed to protecting your privacy. Our Privacy Policy is available online at www.ReaderService.com or upon request from the Harlequin Reader Service.

We make a portion of our mailing list available to reputable third parties that offer products we believe may interest you. If you prefer that we not exchange your name with third parties, or if you wish to clarify or modify your communication preferences, please visit us at www.ReaderService.com/consumerschoice or write to us at Harlequin Reader Service Preference Service, P.O. Box 9062, Buffalo, NY 14269. Include your complete name and address.

HARI3R

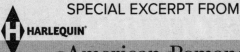
Miranda grinned. Will Dessaro was absolutely adorable when flustered—and he was flustered a lot around her.

How had she coexisted in the same town with him for all these years and not noticed him?

Then came the day of the fire and the order to evacuate within two hours. He'd shown up on her doorstep, strong, silent, capable, and provided the help she'd needed to rally and load her five frightened and uncooperative residents into the van.

She couldn't have done it without him. And he'd been visiting Mrs. Litey regularly ever since.

Thank the Lord her house had been spared. The same couldn't be said for several hundred other homes and buildings in Sweetheart, including many on her own street. Her beautiful and quaint hometown had been brought to its knees in a matter of hours and still hadn't recovered five months later.

"I hate to impose…." Miranda glanced over her shoulder, making sure Will had accompanied her into the kitchen. "There's a leak in the pipe under the sink. The repairman can't fit me in his schedule till Monday, and the leak's worsening by the hour." She paused. "You're good with tools, aren't you?"

"Good enough." He blushed.

Sweet heaven, he was a cutie.

Wavy brown hair that insisted on falling rakishly over one brow. Dark eyes. Cleft in his chin. Breathtakingly tall. He towered above her five-foot-three frame.

If only he'd respond to one of the many dozen hints she'd dropped and ask her on a date.

"Do you mind taking a peek for me?" She gestured toward the open cabinet doors beneath the sink. "I'd really appreciate it."

"Sure." His gaze went to the toolbox on the floor. "You have an old towel or pillow I can use?"

That had to be the longest sentence he'd ever uttered in her presence.

"Be right back." She returned shortly with an old beach towel folded in a large square.

By then, Will had set his cowboy hat on the table and rolled up his sleeves.

Nice arms, she noted. Tanned, lightly dusted with hair and corded with muscles.

She flashed him another brilliant smile and handed him the towel.

His blush deepened.

Excellent. Message sent and received.

Will Miranda lasso her shy cowboy this holiday season?
Find out in
HIS CHRISTMAS SWEETHEART
by New York Times *bestselling author Cathy McDavid*
Available November 5, 2013,
only from Harlequin® American Romance®.

To Love, Honor…and Multiply!

Becoming a husband and family man in the middle of a
raging land feud wasn't the destiny Galen Callahan saw for
himself. But once he laid eyes on Rose Carstairs, he knew
the bouncy blonde with the warrior heart was his future.
Now, with Rancho Diablo under siege, the eldest Callahan
sibling will do whatever it takes to protect his new wife
and triplets. With Callahan lives and legacy on the line,
Galen has a new mission: to vanquish a dangerous enemy
and bring his family together in time for Christmas!

A Callahan Christmas Miracle
by *USA TODAY* bestselling author
TINA LEONARD

Available November 5,
from Harlequin® American Romance®.

American Romance®

A Small Town Thanksgiving
by MARIE FERRARELLA

Ghostwriter Samantha Monroe has just arrived
in Forever, Texas, to turn a remarkable woman's
two-hundred-year-old journals into a personal memoir.
The Rodriguez clan welcomes her with open arms…
and awakens Sam's fierce yearning to be part of a family.
But it's the eldest son, intensely private rancher
Mike Rodriguez, who awakens her passion.

Delving into the past has made Sam hungry for a
future—with Mike. The next move is up to him—if he
doesn't make it, the best woman to ever happen to him
just might waltz back out of his life forever!

**Available November 5,
from Harlequin® American Romance®.**

American Romance®

Christmas Miracles Do Happen!

Cabe Jensen hates Christmas. After losing his beloved wife, the holidays are nothing but a painful reminder of all that was good in his world. When his best friend asks to get married at his ranch, Cabe has no idea that it's to be a Christmas wedding! The worst part is he has to work with Saedra Robbins—a friend of the groom—on the plans.

Trouble is, she's making him feel things he'd rather forget. All Cabe knows is he can't stop thinking about kissing her....

A Cowboy's Christmas Wedding
by PAMELA BRITTON

Available November 5,
from Harlequin® American Romance®.